Before he could even think about what he was doing, he touched her cheek, and it felt right, just like that night.

Just as if he was made to be doing it.

And when Mina turned those green eyes on him, he didn't back away.

Even if every instinct shouted that he should.

Tingles shimmied down Mina's body as she reveled under the feel of Chet's fingers skimming her cheek.

This was how it should be between them—touching, no questions about what was right and wrong, or about office propriety.

He was a man, she was a woman, and right now it was achingly clear that nothing should hold them back from wanting and needing each other.

Or from having a family together.

Dear Reader,

Thank you so much for reading the Billionaire Cowboys, Inc. miniseries! This is the final book in the trilogy, and it's *finally* Chet's turn to find happiness.

He's the illegitimate son who's suffered through the Barron family scandal and, boy, does he need a good woman by his side during this personal crisis. Enter Mina Ferguson, his administrative assistant—and the lady who's been in love with this cowboy ever since she first saw him.

Love at first sight… This is one of my favorite kinds of romances, but not everyone believes it's possible. But what do you think? Does it exist? Has it ever happened to *you?*

I hope this story shows you that love is a blessing—however you find it!

I'd love it if you visited my website at www.crystal-green.com. You can enter contests and see what else I'm up to….

All the best,

Crystal Green

THE TEXAS TYCOON'S BABY

CRYSTAL GREEN

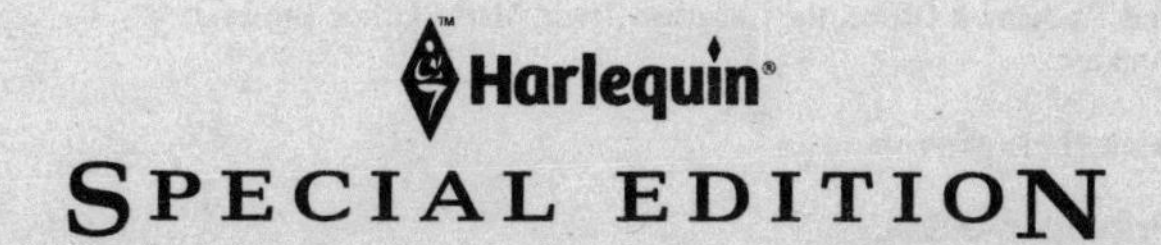

Recycling programs for this product may not exist in your area.

ISBN-13: 978-0-373-65606-6

THE TEXAS TYCOON'S BABY

This edition published by arrangement with Harlequin Books S.A.

For questions and comments about the quality of this book please contact us at Customer_eCare@Harlequin.ca.

www.Harlequin.com

Printed in U.S.A.

Books by Crystal Green

Special Edition

His Arch Enemy's Daughter #1455
**The Stranger She Married* #1498
**There Goes the Bride* #1522
***Her Montana Millionaire* #1574
**The Black Sheep Heir* #1587
The Millionaire's Secret Baby #1668
†*A Tycoon in Texas* #1670
††*Past Imperfect* #1724
The Last Cowboy #1752
The Playboy Takes a Wife #1838
~*Her Best Man* #1850
§*Mommy and the Millionaire* #1887
§*The Second-Chance Groom* #1906
§*Falling for the Lone Wolf* #1932
‡*The Texas Billionaire's Bride* #1981
~~*When the Cowboy Said I Do* #2072
§§*Made for a Texas Marriage* #2093
§§*Taming the Texas Playboy* #2103
§§*The Texas Tycoon's Baby* #2124

Silhouette Romance

Her Gypsy Prince #1789

Silhouette Bombshell

The Huntress #28
Baited #112

Harlequin Blaze

Innuendo #261
Jinxed! #303
"Tall, Dark & Temporary"
The Ultimate Bite #334
One for the Road #387
Good to the Last Bite #426
When the Sun Goes Down #472

*Kane's Crossing
**Montana Mavericks: The Kingsleys
†The Fortunes of Texas: Reunion
††Most Likely To...
~Montana Mavericks: Striking It Rich
§The Suds Club
‡The Foleys and the McCords
~~Montana Mavericks: Thunder Canyon Cowboys
§§Billionaire Cowboys, Inc.

CRYSTAL GREEN

lives near Las Vegas, where she writes for the Harlequin Special Edition and Blaze lines. She loves to read, overanalyze movies and TV programs, practice yoga and travel when she can. You can read more about her at www.crystal-green.com, where she has a blog and contests. Also, you can follow her on Facebook at www.facebook.com/people/Chris-Marie-Green/1051327765 and Twitter at www.twitter.com/ChrisMarieGreen.

To Alicia, Maria and Cindy.
Year after year, decade after decade, we're so lucky that we will always be able to rely on each other!

Prologue

"I'm not who they said I was."

Chet Barron stood in Mina Ferguson's doorway like the walking wounded, his cowboy hat in hand, his short, dark blond hair mussed and out of place. He might've even looked like a bronc buster who'd just been thrown off a wild horse if it wasn't for the gray business suit he had on.

But that was the worse for wear, too; his silk tie was undone, his jacket open to show the wrinkles marring his fine white shirt.

"Chet?" Mina asked.

Shell-shocked, her boss took one step toward her threshold with those Justin Boots—the last vestiges of the cowboy he used to be only eight months ago, before he'd become one of the most powerful tycoons in Texas, if not the entire country.

She took his hand and pulled him the rest of the way

into her home, toward the couch, forgetting about the T-shirt and cutoffs she was wearing—a far cry from the polished skirt suits he usually saw her in.

At the feel of his skin, her pulse jittered, and she knew what would come next—a surge of the blood in her veins. A flip of the belly.

But she knew how to hide how she felt around her boss.

"What's wrong?" she asked as they sat down.

"They lied to me. All these years..."

The cryptic words seemed to freeze in the air.

"What do you mean by that?"

"I mean," he said, his tone still dead, "I'm not his son."

It seemed like a full minute lumbered past.

"I don't understand," Mina said. "Are you talking about Abe? He's...not your father?"

Chet nodded, and when he started to say something else, he choked on the words, burying his face in his hands in a struggle to contain himself.

She exhaled, resting her hand on his arm. Even through his jacket, she felt a burn on her skin, just as she always did when she happened to brush against him while leaning down to set papers on his desk. Or if there happened to be an accidental whisk against each other as they passed in the halls of the offices of the Barron Group.

"It turns out that this was the real reason my dad brought me down here from Montana all those months ago," Chet said, tight sorrow taking hold of his words. "It wasn't just because he had cancer. It wasn't just because he was dying and he wanted me to sell my cattle spread and take his place as CFO of the Group."

Mina kept her hand on his arm, as if she could absorb his hurt. He gripped his hat in both hands as he stared at the floor, his gaze intense.

"Abe told me the whole truth tonight."

When he glanced at Mina, she crumbled inside, because she would do anything to take the obvious agony away from the man she'd loved ever since she'd first met him.

"He wanted me to come to him," Chet said, "so I could take my 'rightful place.' And as the words came out of his mouth, my uncle Eli just stood there next to him with this *look* on his face...."

Chet's words got twisted again, his eyes filled with anger, betrayal.

Out of instinct, Mina put her hand at the back of his head, cradling, soothing, almost thinking *she* could hold a strong man like Chet together.

"Abe told me," he said, "that I was set to inherit a third of the Barron Group, just like my cousins Tyler and Jeremiah. I didn't understand why he and Uncle Eli were going to give me such a big portion when Abe was the minority owner. Then they told me. Eli's my real father. *Eli.*"

His shoulders seemed to lose the steel that had been defining them and he crumbled, his voice gritty with anger and hurt. "My mom had an affair with that bastard years and years ago, and my dad is just telling me now... as he's *dying...*"

Garbled words. Decimated. But he was able to start up again.

"They said that I can claim my damned 'rightful place' now. And I left them standing there because I couldn't hear any more of it."

If a heart could explode, that's what Mina's did. As he fisted his hands, his neck straining with everything he was holding back, she pulled him against her, resting his head on her shoulder, wrapping her arms around him. He encompassed her, too, as if she was some kind of pillar, just as solid as she'd always been for him in the office.

His go-to woman.

But it'd never been like *this* between them, and even though she'd imagined holding him a million times, it wasn't the same now.

She didn't know how long they stayed like that, with him twisting her shirt, pulling at it as he fought emotion, but she heard cars passing by the front window of the tiny house she'd saved up for so diligently, heard the hum of her refrigerator in her kitchen, heard a siren off in the distance.

She didn't pay attention to much of it as his embrace grew tighter and his breath evened out, as she lay her head against his, feeling his thick hair against her face.

He inhaled, a ragged, uneven sound, then shifted, his mouth pressing against her shoulder, where her T-shirt left a patch of skin uncovered, sensitive to every one of his warm breaths.

She couldn't hear anything but her crazed heartbeat, each pump filling her with adrenaline and a growing awareness.

He needed something more.

He needed…

"It'll be okay, Chet," she whispered. "It'll be just fine."

Thuds marked the seconds, beating in her head, and

as she pulled back to look into his gaze, just so he could see that she would make *sure* everything was okay, she recognized a man in the grasp of utter bewilderment.

And then…

Then she leaned into him, pressing her lips to his forehead while cupping his face.

He blinked, his eyes red, but now teeming with something other than raw rage. Hope sprang up in her, sending warmth through every bit of her.

She would make this better. She would do anything to see him smile again.

But then he took her into his arms and pressed his lips to hers so desperately that it robbed her of breath.

Surprise bolted into her. His mouth on hers, the smell of his skin, the urgency in his kiss…

"Mina," he whispered against her lips, as if she'd saved him from the world, even for the moment.

She melted under him, wanting to heal whatever was busted, knowing she was the only one who could comfort him, feeling more alive than ever as the kisses she'd been dreaming of turned to caresses.

As caresses turned into a night that would prove just as fateful as everything that had come before.…

Chapter One

Over Four Months Later

Mina had a secret.

It wasn't obvious, though. Not yet. And she was taking extra care to make sure no one found out about it by wearing a businesslike, no-nonsense skirt and a jacket that covered her stomach—a wardrobe that went along well with the still-warm October weather here in southern Utah.

Yes, she looked just as unruffled as always—or, at least, she was *really* trying to—as she directed traffic in her administrative office at the Red Mountain Escape resort, which the Barron Group was redeveloping and preparing to open in a few months.

"Danny," she said, holding out the newly printed brochure she'd just gone over and marked up.

The young guy, fresh out of college, bounded over to her, snatching the brochure. "What'd you think?"

"Almost there," she said. "But good. Real good."

He gave her a nod then gave way to a second staffer who took his place in front of Mina as she moved away from her desk.

It was Corrine, another hungry and ambitious worker. "I've been around the entire property," the brunette said in a Texas drawl. "Everything's in great shape."

"Everything had better be."

Mina's stomach gave a tumble, but she blew out a breath. *Hold it together,* she kept thinking, as the rest of the staff gathered by the doorway, ready to dart out of it so they could get to their respective posts. *Today of all days, you've got to be the Mina that everyone expects you to be.*

And it wasn't just because progress on everything from the resort's spa to its stables to its recreational facilities and fine-dining restaurant would be subject to the boss's approval when he finally arrived.

Hugging her iPad to her belly, Mina thought of the boss himself.

Chet.

Something in her chest melted at the thought of him. Something in her throat got tight.

For the past months, he'd been on a lot of business trips so he could purchase and then oversee the development of the media holdings and properties that kept the Barron Group flush; trips that had taken him away from the office so he and she had barely been able to see each other for an extended time.

But when they did see each other today, she really had some big news for him.

She fought the sweet urge to cup a hand over her tummy. Four and a half months along. Her stomach hadn't pooched out much, though. Mina had wondered if she should be showing more, but her doctor had assured her that the baby was just the right size and growing. Some women didn't show until later.

But just knowing that she was going to have a baby made her feel as if she was bursting. This would be the first time she would get to really spend time with Chet since she'd gone to the doctor, confirming what she'd begun to suspect after missing her period a couple of times. It'd never been regular, anyway, but in this particular instance, there'd been a reason.

The staff was watching her as if they weren't used to this hesitant version of Mina. She'd always been the efficient one, the one who knew exactly what they should be doing and when.

So she became that woman for them.

"I know every one of you is going to impress Chet when he gets here," she said, avoiding the clock on her desk that counted down to the moment he'd be arriving. "So go to it."

And they did, leaving her alone in her cream leather-and-teakwood office, which sat right next door to the one Chet would occupy.

Even without him there, she felt him.

But, really, *wasn't* he with her in a sense?

She adjusted her jacket over her tummy as nerves surged through her. The last thing she wanted to do was tell him she was expecting, and that's why she'd been putting it off for as long as she could while he was off on all those business trips. That family scandal of his had done its work, chipping away at him until he was only a shell of the man she'd fallen for all those months ago, when he'd first appeared at the Group's offices.

How would a man who was having such issues with his illegitimate birth react to the news that he was having an out-of-wedlock baby?

A car's beeping horn tugged at her attention, and she went to her long window, where a view of the pure blue Utah sky and the ridges of the claylike mountains reached toward the heavens.

Her pulse started jogging double-time now, but it wasn't exactly the breathtaking scenery that did it.

In the near distance, Chet emerged from the back of a town car, shutting the door without waiting for the driver to do it for him. He sauntered over the stone-lined path leading to the offices, his cowboy hat pulled low over his brow, his shoulders wide, his chest broad under a long-sleeved Western shirt. He walked like a man in charge of everything around him, but from the way his gaze was shadowed, Mina knew better. Even from here she could imagine the darkness that turned his blue irises to a midnight hue, that made him resemble a mysterious—and dangerous—man huddled in the corner of an Old West bar, one hand near his holster, the other resting near a half-empty drinking glass.

Just a glimpse of him made Mina go weak, light and floaty in a nerve-racked way that also caused her to feel more alive than ever before in her life. A little sob wrestled itself down in her—she was so glad to see him. So scared.

Now that they'd be spending some quality time together, she would have to choose the right moment to tell him her news.

If there was a right moment…

He disappeared from her view, entering the administrative building, and her heartbeat got louder, as if the ground was vibrating and sending thunder through her veins.

All she could think about was that night… Or, more to the point, the moments after they'd made love, when the world had come crashing down around her.

But now wasn't the time to think of that, especially when she heard him at her doorway.

She exhaled once more, turning around and telling herself not to look as if she had a secret that might send him running.

"Long time, no real see," he said, leaning against the door frame, grinning, as if he was happy to confirm that she'd made it here from San Antonio safely a few days ago when he'd sent her ahead to inspect the property before he arrived.

Mina's insides did something like a thousand individual back bends, tying her up.

Was it because there was something in his gaze? A *pow* that turned the dark blue of his cycs into a second of firework brightness?

Was he remembering how perfect they'd been for each other just when he'd needed someone to hold him and ease him?

Mina had seen the same *pow* in him a couple of times since then, during car rides to or from the airport where she would debrief him on the run, or during their frequent long-distance teleconferences. But she could never be sure.

They'd never mentioned that night again. And she'd never told him that the condom he'd worn hadn't worked.

"How was the flight?" she asked.

"Just fine. I can't stand being cooped up though, even if I'm taking the corporate jet. There's something about being in an enclosed place, especially thousands of feet in the air where I don't have the choice of getting out."

"Sounds like a man who misses the open range."

He smiled, doffing his hat and holding it by his side, as if remembering the old days, before Abe had called him down to Texas from the comfort of a Montana cattle operation. Chet had sold his holdings to go to work for the Barron Group—a move that he'd made after finding out about Abe's cancer.

That was even before Abe had told Chet about his true parentage though, before his world had broken open. Mina couldn't imagine what that kind of news would do to anyone—making them doubt all the truths a person had ever known, shattering their trust in the people they depended on for honesty.

Abe had died a few months ago, further adding to Chet's sorrows, taking away the man he'd thought to be his father for a second time in under a year.

As he tossed his hat on a nearby wingback chair, Mina wondered if there'd ever be a right time to put another life-changing piece of news in front of him.

She slid her iPad onto her desktop, then made her way over, standing before him, not sure whether to hug him in greeting or not. Memory halted her as she recalled the heartbreaking aftermath of that night: how the lamplight had bathed them as they lay on that couch, her clothes on the floor, her skin singing with the afterburns of his touch, her body aching pleasantly after being filled with him.

Mina, he'd said, and she'd caught trouble in his tone. She'd held her breath as her giddiness—her bliss at how they'd finally come together—dissipated.

I took advantage of you...

As she'd reeled under that, he started talking about how he knew she wanted to be a serious businesswoman, and he'd never meant to cast a shadow on her reputation. He didn't want everyone to think that she owed her career to her sex life with him.

Even then, she'd known that he was talking around the real issues—how he couldn't handle a relationship in all the turmoil that'd come to him that night, how he'd let his anger and grief get the better of him. And every bit of it had rung through her like a punch that had deadened her chest, then the rest of her body.

He had no idea that she would've given up everything—a career, her solid reputation—for his love.

But with the way he'd looked into her eyes, as if he hated himself and was confused about everything around him, she had forgiven him. It was beyond her to despise him when she'd freely offered comfort. And even though it had torn her apart to say it, she'd told him that everything was okay between them—no harm, no foul. From there, he'd gone his way and she'd gone hers, always his stalwart. Always his girl, even if he didn't know it.

She'd thought about quitting her job, just so she wouldn't have to torture herself any longer, but the thought of being away from him was even worse. And they *had* been able to work with each other in the aftermath, thank goodness. Yes, she'd mostly stayed at their San Antonio headquarters while he'd traveled around the country on various projects, but there'd been one exception to that—when they'd spent a day at his brother Tyler's wedding. She'd only been at the festivities because she'd worked with the oldest Barron brother for years and she'd been invited. Chet hadn't asked her to accompany him.

Besides, that had been before the doctor had given her the official word about her pregnancy.

Now, as she stood in front of him, so unsure about how to act, Chet looked just as out of sorts as ever, his gaze searching hers.

Then he laid a hand on her arm, as if that was a good enough greeting.

Her skin tingled, even under the cotton of her blouse. She could feel the weight of his hand even after he removed it and wandered farther into her office, heading toward the window to take in that mountain view.

Just let him get his head together a little longer, Mina thought as dismay needled her. *Wait until he's in a better place to hear that he's going to be a dad, because if you tell him at the wrong time or in the wrong way you'll lose him completely.*

She went to the window to stand by him. Even though he had moments where she believed he was so damaged by what had gone on with his family, there were times when she thought he could come around, especially here, in the desert, away from the drama. This ranch spa was his dream, and a distraction, too. He was putting his heart and soul into renovating it, and it was almost as though, if he could build this place back up, he could do the same with himself.

Even with the positive thoughts, though, something niggled at Mina. What if she *had* only been there to cushion his fall that night, and she really didn't mean any more to him than that? Chet was the type who would marry a woman he'd gotten pregnant purely out of honor. But honor wouldn't be enough in a marriage.

And Mina didn't want that from him. She wanted his love. Her child deserved that, too. Mina knew exactly what it was like to be a surprise baby—she'd been an "accidental child," as well, except her own mom and dad had been very married.

She'd just been a "happy" accident for them during a hard financial time that they'd eventually recovered from. At least, that's what she'd overheard from a drunk uncle talking about it during a barbecue years and years ago.

Even now the thought stung as she and Chet stood at that window. Both of them, accidents. She related more to him than he knew.

She wished she could just reach out and touch him. She was dying to.

But she didn't.

While he surveyed the property, she could just about feel the pride radiating off of him. So many things in his life were messed up, but this resort wouldn't be one of them.

"It's going to be amazing," she said, a catch in her voice, because she wasn't just talking about the property.

"I aim to make it that way." He glanced at her, and her pulse skipped. "I hear we're scheduled to have the chef show off her menu tonight."

"In your cabin. I arranged a tasting for you."

"Just me?"

She hesitated. What did he mean?

"Please," he said lightly, "tell me you won't make

me test that menu alone. I'm counting on your opinion about how everything is shaping up here."

"I was going to get around to a tasting."

"Get it over with tonight. We'll catch up over dinner. We haven't been able to have a real sit-down in a long time."

There was a gleam in his eyes that she couldn't quite translate. Was he finally ready to be with her one-on-one again? Not even necessarily in a romantic manner, but just as friends?

"I guess I could use a good meal and a break," she said, determined to take charge of this relationship, to show him that she could always be there, along with a family who would love him through thick and thin.

"Good." He smiled, almost to himself, as he hitched his thumbs in his jeans pockets. "I was also thinking that you might want to take a horseback tour of the property with me right now."

When she'd been to the OB-GYN, she'd asked about exercising, as she did it regularly. Jogging, a calm horse ride, some light Pilates… But her doc wasn't a fan of riding during pregnancy, and she wasn't about to do anything to endanger her child.

"How about a walking tour instead?" she asked.

"Okay then." He backed away from the window, and really, his blue gaze was clearer than she'd seen it in a while. Was it because he was out here…or because *she* was here?

She could only wish.

He moved toward the doorway, scooping his hat back up and putting it on—a rough and rugged man who would surprise anyone if they were to see him in a business suit, looking slightly out of place, yet dashing just the same.

Mina even jellied a bit in the knees at the thought of him dressed up.

"You ready?" he asked.

God, if he only knew just how ready she was. She wished he had even an inkling of how much she wanted him to stroll off into the sunset with her.

She thought she saw that spark in his gaze again as he glanced at her, and optimism wove its way under her skin. Was it possible that he would see how much she adored him before she told him about their child?

Would it make a difference if she could show him that she wanted more than just a night with him?

Only time would tell, she thought as she went to the door.

He ushered her out of the office as her heart stuck in her throat.

They sauntered side by side on a trail that headed toward thc hills, cutting through thc stillncss of thc latc afternoon.

It was actually nice to get away from the office, even though staying busy was good, Chet thought.

Very good.

While passing the scrub and barrel cactus at the foot of some red-tinged hills, he did his best to keep his mind off of everything—including his assistant. Thank God they'd settled back into an amiable pattern, especially after that night when he'd overstepped his bounds with her.

What had he been thinking, coming on to Mina? He'd never been so unprofessional in his life. In fact, he imagined that taking advantage of an employee was something a womanizer like his biological father, Eli Barron, might've done in the past.

But that wasn't Chet. Hell, no. He respected women, Mina more than most of them. And when he thought about what might happen if word about them ever got out around the Barron Group, he wanted to throttle himself.

She was ambitious, wanted to build a career. But was everyone going to think that she'd slept her way to the top?

Luckily, she'd been gracious and accepting of his errors, not holding Chet to any promises that his body might've made to her. Maybe he should've given her up, hired another personal assistant, but he wasn't about to punish her for his lack of judgment that night.

And she was too damned good at her job for him to give her up, too.

Besides, they'd worked things out. Certainly, it involved him traveling a lot, but he was getting a lot done for the Group, buying up land and property then renovating and building on it to add the Group's coffers. So it was a decent trade-off. He'd cleared his head quite a bit, and enough time had passed that they could go back to being…

What? What *had* they been to each other?

The wind carried a hint of Mina's perfume past him, and it made him light-headed, reminding him of what it felt like when he'd held her against him.

When he'd first seen her as more than an assistant.

That night he'd filled himself up with the scent of her, a combination of green tea and…calm. It was at odds with her sunset hair, which seemed so very lively against the quiet of the desert as the breeze cajoled a stray lock out of her upswept hairdo.

In spite of all his efforts, Chet stole an even better peek at her now. Wearing a skirt that came to her knees, she had the posture and the elegance of a lady, with high cheekbones sprinkled with freckles and clover-hued eyes that usually bore a sparkle.

But there wasn't much of a sparkle today. In fact, there was some kind of distance.

Did seeing him again for more than a debriefing make her think about what had happened between them?

Disappointment clawed at him, surprising him with its sharpness. From the way they'd fallen back into their boss-assistant relationship, he could've sworn that she'd let go of that night. Hell, he would've even said that she'd been relieved when he'd told her that he should've never put her in a position to assuage his anguish.

Even now, he still wanted to kick himself for how he'd acted with her after he'd held her, kissed her, been inside of her.

I'm sorry...I took advantage of you...

He just hadn't known what to make of what had happened. His emotions had been abraded, bleeding, and she'd been there. That's all.

And it had been wrong to pull her into his vortex of trouble.

How was it that he'd ruined so many things in his life without trying? Mina, and even his family. He hadn't meant to be born the way he was, but the truth of his birth had thrown everyone into chaos, anyway, and as ridiculous as it seemed, he felt responsible.

Rocks crunched under their boots. The silence between them was like a saw, and he had to turn it off.

"Where are we off to first?" he asked.

"How about the spa?" She motioned to the east where, just over the hills, the white dome of the building peeked up. Around it, there would be pools with waterfalls and serene sculptures.

Mina added, "You should see the inside. There's a meditation room with floor-to-ceiling windows, and a quiet lounge with fountains where the guests will go while waiting for their treatments. You should see the Paradise Room, too, with its waterfall and pool."

She seemed fine with the small talk, just as she was fine with everything.

When her phone rang, the sound split the air. She took it out of her pocket and glanced at her ID screen, then put it away.

"It's my mom. She's probably calling to chat." She laughed. "Or, should I say, to check up on me."

He knew from comments Mina had made here and there that her family was really tight. They had frequent get-togethers at her parents' home in the San Antonio suburbs, with her two local sisters and their brood usually in attendance.

Odd that he knew so little about her private life when she seemed to know so much about his because of the scandal.

"How's the family doing?" he asked.

"Great. Same as always—caring, nosy, all that."

Was there some dryness in the way she'd said it?

"You're not too keen on the nosy part," he said.

"Not really, but what family isn't that way? It just means they care about what happens to me."

Her words struck Chet hard. He'd been doing everything possible to avoid anything even near to "nosy" or "involved" with his own family. Then again, they weren't much like the Fergusons at all. First, there was Eli, who'd been hitting the bottle hard ever since he and Abe had announced that Chet was Eli's son. Then there were his brothers, who were doing their best to deal with the situation in their own ways.

The term "family" didn't really even apply to the lot of them. Actually, Chet wasn't sure what a family was since his own had obviously been a lie. His mother had passed on a few years ago in a car accident with Aunt Florence, who supposedly hadn't known about her sister-in-law's affair with Eli.

And Mom wasn't the woman he'd thought she was.

That left Abe.

Something in Chet's core took a fall at the thought of him. The man he'd called "Dad." The man he'd abandoned for a life in Montana just as soon as he was old enough to get out of the house and strike out on his own.

And Chet had *wanted* to leave because, intuitively, he'd always suspected there was something off whenever Abe and his mom had exchanged those heavy, sad glances when they thought "their son" hadn't been looking.

But there were other reasons Chet didn't want to be with his new family right now. Abe's recent death had made it hard. And how much *did* Chet have to do with Abe's passing? Had the truth weighed on his "father" so roughly that it'd helped to kill Abe?

Remorse bit at Chet once again. He only wished Abe were still alive. So many things to make up for. So many things that had been thrust upon Chet now that the truth had come out…

The desert breeze sidled up to him again, along with the scent of Mina. Chet kept his gaze on the path as a bird of prey cried overhead, and his mind went fuzzy, making him forget everything, just for a moment.

But then he sensed Mina watching him and his heart kicked as his gaze connected to hers.

She looked away, but not before he thought he glimpsed a wounded look in her eyes.

Was she more affected by that night than she let on?

Chet felt every cell in his body screaming. Yet what could he say to her?

That night, I did need you, and you were there for me. You were the best thing that could've ever happened...

A vibration shook his shirt pocket and, at first, Chet mistook it for another memory—of the way she'd grabbed hold of his heart, his entire being, and shocked both of them to life.

But when the vibration came again, he knew it was merely *his* phone now.

Mina grinned. "Not a moment of rest for us, even out in the boonies."

Her smile was like a warming beacon, and he only answered the phone because it was Tyler's number, and his cousin's—or, rather, brother's—calls were rarely unimportant.

Putting the phone to his ear, he said, "Hey, Tyler."

Mina walked on a few steps ahead of him, giving him privacy.

Tyler was already talking. "You have an ETA for when you'll be back in Texas?"

"I just got to St. George. Why?"

Tyler paused for one of those quiet moments that he'd used so well as the big boss of the Barron Group before he'd retired to start up a horse rescue with his new wife, Zoe. Back when Chet had first started working at the Group, he'd welcomed Tyler's competitive guidance. The same for Jeremiah, his slightly older brother.

But out here, Chet felt very much alone, especially with Mina strolling ahead, her back to him, her hips swaying under that skirt.

He forced himself to look away. "Is it Eli again?"

"Sure enough. He went on a real bender last night. Tore up the lounge at the Broadway, and our lawyers had to step in to run interference."

Chet wanted to throw the phone, but he kept himself contained. "The last time we were all together, he told us that he was going to change." They'd been planning an intervention, but when Eli had vowed he was turning a corner, they'd trusted him.

"He was wrong." Tyler paused. "Jeremiah and I confronted him, then helped him check in to the Whitehall Center for rehab."

Chet felt his shoulders stiffen.

"But," Tyler added, "I won't rush you to get back here because of that, Chet. He can't have visitors right now. It'd just be good if you could come back when he's improved enough to see us. Maybe it'll even happen around the time of Jeremiah's wedding."

"You know I'll be there for that."

But as for visiting Eli?

Damn it, Chet knew he should be anticipating the day it would be possible. Still, he held back the rest of what he wanted to say to Tyler—that if it was Abe instead of Eli who was in trouble, Chet wouldn't have gone out of town at all; he would have been around to help Tyler and Jeremiah deal with him. And if Eli hadn't been so selfish when he'd had the affair with Chet's mother—and if he wasn't being so self-centered now—it would've been so much easier to accept him.

Plus, Chet mentally added, it would've been easier to accept himself, too, because he was Eli's son now, and he wondered how much he'd inherited from the man he didn't really know.

"I'll check in tomorrow about my ETA," Chet finally said.

They both signed off. When Chet hung up, he stared at the mountains for a moment, feeling aimless.

Then he realized that Mina was waiting for him and for a moment—just a heartwarming flash—he allowed her to comfort him again.

Knowing he would have to rely on more than this to get him through the next months, he forced the dark look that he knew he must've been wearing off of his face and walked over to her.

As she faced him with those compassionate green eyes, he sank into another memory of that night, memories that always came unbidden whenever he saw her.

Holding her, because he didn't know what else to grab on to. Running his hands over her soft, smooth skin, her waist and hips, just before he entered the warmth of her…

His belly seized up, hot and sharp, but he pushed back the sensation. Again.

"Everything okay?" she asked, searching his gaze. There was something more intense about her than usual, though he couldn't put his finger on it.

Not wanting to lay anything more on her than he

already had, he nodded. "Ty was just putting things in order with the family."

A strange look crossed her expression. Was it because he was shutting her out of a more complete answer?

As she moved on, Chet frowned, wondering if they'd left that night behind after all.

Chapter Two

After showering, Chet felt a hell of a lot better. Good enough to kick back with a beer in his cabin near the main lodge before the chef would arrive with dinner.

And before Mina would get here, too.

Once more, an inexplicable warmth surrounded Chet's heart. All he'd done was just think of her.

What was going on with him?

Desperate to clear his head, he wandered to the outside deck, where a few hardy chairs and a stone fire pit offered welcome. Later that week, a designer would start putting the grace notes on the guest cabins, as well as the main lodge itself. He and Mina were scheduled to leave the resort in a matter of days—too many other projects to oversee, such as a renovated art-deco office building in New York, a condo project near the Vegas Strip, a grand hotel on the Florida coast. But they'd be back before the grand opening of this one.

As he leaned on the rail, his beer bottle dangling from his fingers, the A-frame of the cabin loomed, all rising glass windows and reaching upper deck—a rustic retreat for the rich clientele who would visit this resort for spa and adventure getaways.

A sense of pride welled within him as he took another drink. It felt good to be building something up rather than tearing it down.

Soon, the chef and her staff came, armed with covered trays, along with enough matched wines to keep a person going for weeks. He stayed outside while they prepared his table.

When he saw Mina coming down the path to his cabin, his blood rushed through his veins again.

There was no fighting it.

She'd pulled her auburn hair, with its sleekly styled layers, away from her flushed face so that the rest of it fell to her shoulders. The hairdo revealed a graceful neck and jawline, plus those cheekbones. Closer up, he knew that her thick lashes would be so long that a princess would kill for them. And the princess imagery didn't stop there—she was wearing a white peasant's camisole and yellow skirt that swished just over feet dressed in simple yet elegant sandals. With that stately posture of hers, she seemed like some kind of royal miss who was running off from the castle for an evening to be with him—the pauper, not the prince.

Or, at least, that was what he felt like, even though the Barrons had made him a rich, successful billionaire just like his brothers. Still, Chet didn't know how he fit in to their lives...his *own* new one, too. He felt as if...

Well, as if he was still on the outside, no matter

how hard Tyler and Jeremiah tried to make him feel differently.

Why couldn't he have been Abe's son through and through? Why had Eli been so irresponsible, creating him—a bastard who didn't really belong, no matter what his parentage was?

Mina's voice eased into his thoughts. "I got a special delivery a half hour ago."

She'd been holding something behind her back, and now she revealed the object: a small basketball hoop with a spongy ball, just like the one he had back in the San Antonio office.

He couldn't help but smile.

Mina's pale skin flushed, as if appreciating his response. "You're always saying that your office here—and even your cabin—lack a personal touch. I thought I'd take a step in remedying that."

"I guess it's obvious that I'm not so good at sitting still." Even when he was supposed to be kicking back with his boots on the desk and thinking. The motion of arcing a basketball—foam or not—through the air and getting all net gave him a measure of serenity. Not many other people knew that much about him.

She ascended the stairs to the deck and set the sports gear on a chair. His gut tied itself into knots as he thought of what it'd felt like to run his fingers over those bare arms, long, slender, pale, soft. He remembered what her skin had tasted like, too…

When her gaze caught his, it seemed to flare with the same desire he was feeling.

Her lips parted as if she wanted to say something.

But then the basketball backboard slid off the chair and hit the deck, making them both start.

They laughed awkwardly. She might've even been just as relieved as he was for the interruption.

Laughing. It was something he would have to do more. Sometimes he wondered what had happened to the old him—the guy who used to shoot the bull and laugh with his pals at the Watering Hole near his Montana ranch.

Where had that normal life gone?

And, worse yet, he wasn't even sure if the new him would ever be able to laugh, relax, trust people as he used to.

It was the trust part that worried him the most.

"Thanks for the special delivery," he said, raising his beer bottle to her, thinking that, if there was anyone to be trusted now, it was definitely Mina. "Care for a drink before dinner?"

"I'll have water when we get inside," she said.

"You usually like wine during dinner."

Her skin was really flushed now. "It's the desert. I feel…dehydrated."

"Then I'll be a proper host and get that water for you now." He motioned for her to take a seat in one of the chairs then went to scoop the backboard and ball from the ground. "Be right back."

She didn't protest when he went to get an ice-filled glass of water. He put down the sports items by the stone fireplace and came back out to see her face raised to the last of the turquoise sky, streaks of pale color etching it to dusk.

He handed her the beverage, and when she drank, he watched her lips—the lushness, the way her mouth tilted slightly up at the corners, as if it couldn't help smiling.

She leaned her head back. "I can smell the food from out here. It makes the place seem like home, doesn't it? Good food, I mean. All that's missing is a table weighed down with a week's worth of grub and my mom telling us that we need to take as many leftovers home as we can carry."

Chet let her description of home wash over him.

Then she sighed.

"What?" he asked.

"Nothing."

"That was a sigh for the ages, Mina. It didn't mean 'nothing.'"

She cocked her eyebrow at him. "Sometimes I think it's not a good thing that you can read me, boss."

Boss. It gave him some firmer footing with her.

He rested the beer bottle on the wooden railing. "People don't sigh unless there's something worth sighing about."

She waved her hand, as if dismissing something. "It's just… Well, that call from Mom today. Even though I'm twenty-eight, sometimes I feel like I'm still a teenager, and I can't go a few days without filing a report about my doings. She says that single girls like me need to have someone check in with them, just to see that they haven't fallen down and can't get up in their house or… whatever emergencies go through a mom's mind. She doesn't like that there's no one else around most of the time."

"You're the light of her life."

"I know… She loves me." Mina grinned. "And I know she's right about checking in with me. Still, sometimes I just want to untangle myself from my family a little. They have a tendency to overstep."

"And that chaps your hide."

She laughed at his colorful description. "Family's always going to be there through thick and thin when others might not be. That's the bottom line. I'll even withstand my mom's phone calls for that."

He thought of his own mom: how she'd betrayed his dad but still loved her son way up in Montana. She used to call him, too, fussing over him, making sure he realized he always had someone somewhere who loved him, even though it was far across the miles. And now he knew why she'd put out the extra effort—to make it up to him because, one day, he might know the truth about what she had done to him and Abe.

So *much* of it had been a lie.

Mina said, "I love having a mom—don't get me wrong. But she feels like she also..."

Trailing off, Mina took another drink, as if she regretted even bringing this up.

"She what?" Chet asked.

Mina got that look on her face that she usually adopted when she was balancing the consequences of something. Then she lowered her glass, holding it with both hands on her lap.

"My parents have this guilt trip when it comes to me, and my mom sometimes overcompensates." She got that expression again—the measuring, the hesitation. "I was never supposed to come along. I was a surprise for my parents."

As she watched him, Chet didn't move a muscle. Even after he'd learned about his own birthright, Mina had never told him this piece of news. And it'd probably been because of what'd gone on between them...because of how he'd let her down afterward and damaged their friendship, taking away their former closeness, which was just beginning to return now.

But he was ready to mend what he'd broken, and damned if he wasn't going to make great strides in it tonight.

She glanced away, yet he could see that her gaze was bruised. No one wanted to be an accidental baby.

"We have more in common than you ever expected, don't we?" she asked. "My circumstances are hardly the same as yours, but when I found out that I was just sort of thrust into this world without a plan, it pushed me to a place where I felt pretty alone for a while. My parents never even knew that I stumbled on the truth, but it sure shaped me, just as it's shaping you in a way."

"Shaping me," he said slowly.

"Yeah. I think it's what made *me* such a pleaser—you know the type." Her smile was wistful. "The Girl Fridays of the world, the ones who have to make sure everyone is happy with them. I spent years being the secretary of the school's governance team and every childhood club on my block, honing my skills at being the go-to person."

"So that's why you're so good at your job." And making herself relevant to others. When he'd found out that he'd come from the wrong side of the blanket, he'd felt as if he didn't have much of a place in the Texas Barron family, even though Eli had tried like hell to fit him into the company, making him a co-vice president right off the bat.

"Maybe you're right." She grew quiet, as if she had so much more to say but didn't know how to word it.

Chet even got the feeling that there was something

going on here that he would never understand, something deep in her that she wouldn't reveal easily.

And it scared him that he cared enough to know just what it was.

He tried to figure out a way to bring up the subject but was stopped short by Chef Arnett coming to the sliding glass door in her whites and announcing that dinner was ready to be served.

Going to Mina's deck chair, Chet offered her a hand, helping her up. Her flesh branded his and he backed off sooner than he meant to, recovering by ushering her ahead of him inside, where, in the living area, a fountain ran through the room. The water sculpture had been designed to recall a Japanese garden, with stone lanterns and raked rocks surrounding a pond that would hold koi fish when it came closer to the grand opening of the ranch.

They arrived at the dining space, a stone table with padded silk chairs. A lone candle burned in the midst of the settings. A bottle of wine rested in a silver bucket of ice, but when Chet went to pour it, Mina refused him again.

"I'm sticking with the water," she said, refilling her glass with the pitcher resting on the table.

As they sat, Chef Arnett folded her hands in front of her, smiling. Chet could tell that the young apple-cheeked woman was nervous about serving the big bosses.

"I've prepared sample dishes—tasting portions," she said, sliding two menus onto the table so they could see what was in store. "Five courses, and they're all made in the spirit of good health." Just like the resort would be promoting.

"Hellfire," Chet said, perusing the list. Like the menu of the San Francisco restaurant from which they'd recruited Chef Arnett, there were a lot of choices. Even after so many months of this life change—from rancher to business tycoon—he wasn't used to the luxuries.

They thanked her, and when she left them to enjoy the first course, they started with a choice of appetizers. Chet dug in to what the chef called a crab rémoulade salad paired with a Chenin Blanc wine, which Mina, of course, didn't want.

That's when Chet realized what might be going on. Was she actually afraid of dropping her defenses with him? Was she afraid that they might do something they regretted again, out here away from the office?

It was time to get everything in the clear.

"Are you angry with me, Mina?"

She put down her fork and lifted her linen napkin, dabbing at her mouth. It seemed to take forever as Chet waited.

"Angry?" she asked.

"For what happened after we were together."

She cleared her throat. "No. Of course I'm not angry."

"Good. Because you know there are reasons it had to end there."

"I know your reasons."

She lifted her gaze, and even though her green eyes were clear, there were depths that he couldn't fathom.

He added, "I told you that I'd hate for word to get around the Group that you were with the boss, so I've been standoffish. Maybe too much."

Blinking, Mina paused, as if she'd expected him to say something else, though he wasn't sure what.

But, hell, he *did* care about her ambitions, and if everyone knew that they'd been together, it would mark her, undermine her true talents.

Yet was that really the only reason he wanted to set their relationship back to rights?

Chet shut down the possibility of there being any more between them while waiting for his Girl Friday to respond.

Mina's head fizzed with confusion.

Was this the time to give him the news about the baby, now that they were getting matters out into the open?

A gnawing feeling told her that she should just stay quiet at this point.

One step at a time. They were doing well so far, getting back onto normal ground with each other.

She met Chet's blue gaze again, bracing herself for the impact that always hit her whenever he was close, and—*boom*. Stomach somersaulting, the acrobatics in her chest… They didn't disappoint, leaving her nearly breathless.

He looked serious, so she sat still, as if something was about to crack between them, like a piece of glass they'd been tiptoeing over.

He gazed at her a tension-filled moment longer, then shook his head. "Just look at us. Things are so thick in the air that I can practically carve it. And I'll be damned if our work suffers because of it."

Her heart sank so low that it might as well have crumbled to nothing. Maybe there really wouldn't be a future between them…

For the first time, panic hit her.

Was she going to be a single mom? Her—the woman who'd been so together?

She also had to admit that all the family talk from earlier had done a number on her, and she was extra sensitive right now. After chatting with her mom today, she'd started really thinking about how her nearest and dearest would react to Chet, the scandal-plagued man who'd been wreaking havoc on her. Her family would be real protective of Mina for certain, just as they'd been after her last significant other had broken her heart.

That's probably why she'd been so put out about her mom checking up on her today, when it normally didn't bother her as much. Facing Chet had just exacerbated her emotions.

"I'm only hoping I didn't damage our relationship permanently," Chet added.

"You haven't. We haven't." Mina reached for a piece of fresh bread from the basket.

"It's just..." He lost his words, then picked them back up. "Do you remember when talk used to come easier between us? We used to kid each other, like about how I never went on dates. And I'd do the same to you. These days, the very subject would take on new meaning."

"You think that we'd be keeping each other in check or something? That there'd still be strings attached to us just because of one night?"

"Don't you think so?"

One of the chef's assistants peeked out from around the corner, gauging their reaction to the first part of the meal. When Mina caught her eye, the young ponytailed woman drew back.

This wasn't exactly the perfect place for a life-altering kind of talk, Mina thought.

She gestured toward his salad. "What do you think so far?"

Chet's broad shoulders sank, as if he'd wanted to talk more. "Top-notch."

They continued eating. She suddenly noticed that Chef Arnett had even selected some music to go with the meal. Beethoven. The chaotic symphony did little to calm her racing thoughts.

"So," he said, as if he couldn't help himself. "After we get the resort manager in place, you'll have a breather from this project and the office altogether. I'll see to it. You've been running yourself ragged lately."

"I like working."

"I think you work too much sometimes."

"Look who's talking."

He grinned at that. "Look, indeed."

After a few more minutes, Chef Arnett appeared again, this time with more samples and paired wines: things like parmesan-crusted scallops, pan-seared salmon over risotto, grilled poussin with fingerling potatoes. At the delicious aroma, Mina wanted to dig in. Her appetite was growing by the week, but there was no way she would let Chet see that.

When the chef was gone, Chet continued, "All I'm saying is that I'm afraid business has taken over your life."

"Wrong."

At his quirked eyebrow, she realized what he was getting around to.

Was he attempting to see if she'd moved on from him? If she was "getting out of the office" with a social life, which might or might not include another man?

Well, wouldn't that be a nice break for Chet—her

falling for a different guy, one who was emotionally available. But it was disheartening, because he had to have felt *something* on that night—something that had stayed with him as much as it'd stayed with her. She knew it because of the way he'd touched her, whispered her name as if it was carrying him to a new, better place.

She'd never heard a man say her name like that before.

"I'll tell you what," she said, capturing a forkful of creamed spinach. "I'll hop right on to an internet social-networking site once we're done here and attempt to find some sort of real life if that'll make you feel any better."

All he did was smile again, appreciating her feistiness.

"What's so funny?" she asked.

"A man doesn't have to be told to back off of a conversation much more clearly than that, Mina."

Okay. Being defensive with him wasn't going to get them back on track, or to where she could measure how he was going to take the pregnancy news.

"It's just that it's—" she was still holding that spinach-topped fork "—been a while. For a relationship, I mean."

"Me, too."

"I know. You dated back in Montana but never got serious. And you've had a dry spell here because of all the drama. I have access to your social calendar, remember?"

"You have the advantage over me then. I don't know a thing about yours."

There was something in his tone that hinted he was truly interested, and Mina's heart bumped her chest.

"I haven't booked many dates for a while," she said, giving in, testing him further. "And it's probably for the best."

She ate the spinach.

"What was he like?" Chet asked. "Your last relationship?"

This was good, Mina thought. Chet showing a burst of curiosity about her personal life.

Did it mean he cared beyond just friendship?

She watched him carefully. "Michael was one of those free spirits. Reluctant to settle down, even though I kept thinking he was going to change his mind one day. Eventually, I realized that I wanted more from a man, and he didn't want more from a woman, so I did what was best for the both of us and broke it off." She put down her fork and wrapped her fingers around her cool glass of water. "Months of my life wasted. But I had time to recover, seeing as it ended about a year ago."

And then Chet had come along. From that moment on, she'd known that he was the one, and every other man she'd ever known had only been a lead-up to the real thing.

Her boss toasted her with his wine. "Good thing, then, that your family was there for you, for comfort and some shoulders to lean on."

As he drank, she realized that he was referring to their earlier discussion outside on the deck. And that there was a longing in his voice that he couldn't cover up.

Mina reached across the table, resting her hand on

his. When the contact sizzled, making both her and Chet start, she removed her touch.

Patience, she thought. *Don't rush things.*

"I'm glad to hear you say that about family." She fiddled with the napkin on her lap. If she kept her hands busy, maybe she wouldn't reach for him again.

"I'm sorting through my situation more and more." There was something in his voice—a break? Was it because she'd touched him? "There're just plenty of questions to deal with, like who my mom really was. And if I even *want* to be Eli Barron's son."

"I guess you do have a choice in that."

"Sure. I could still act like I'm Abe's and I could let Eli know that there's no chance that I'll ever be like a son to him. But that would be destructive when Eli's already in a black hole." He rested his hand on his wineglass. "That phone call earlier today, when I talked to Tyler? He told me that he and Jeremiah helped Eli into rehab."

Her heart almost broke at how much sadness cut into his apparent relief. "That's a good thing."

"Yeah. It is."

Just listen to him. He was worrying about Eli, even though the man should pay for the destruction he'd done to his own family.

Yes, Chet had a heart. He was a good man who would no doubt be a good father and, maybe someday, a good husband. But as they fell into more silence, Mina wondered just when he was going to realize that about himself, if ever.

Chef Arnett returned to bring a few more samples, which gave them the opportunity to heap praise on her. By the time they were ready for dessert, Chet was leaning back in his chair, looking more relaxed than he had in a long time.

Mina leaned back, too, her optimism revving up full force.

The time *would* come, she thought. She just needed to wait a bit longer.

They'd called it an early night, knowing that the next day would hold some major work, with contractors on-site to get the ranch going before its opening date as well as a few final candidates who would meet with Mina about the managerial position. Chet knew that she'd screened them beforehand, whittling them down to this elite group.

His day would consist of appointments with a few local ranches, where he intended to check out horse stock. But before he left the resort, he would have to check in with Mina about a locals preview night that they would be staging tomorrow: giving tours of the property, handing out samples of the cuisine and entertaining the crowd with music.

Thinking this would be a good time to take a more casual look at the resort's progress, he made his way to the main lodge, with its combination of Native American artwork and Asian-inspired comforts, such as the silk cushions that lined the furniture and the rock gardens that led to the reception dome.

There, he found Mina going over last-minute details for the glass-and-cedar decor that would distinguish this area.

The same shock-and-rock sensation he felt whenever he saw her rattled him. She had her hair in a French braid, and she was garbed in a smart, short-sleeved cool blue suit as she took charge with the contractor. When they were done, she checked her iPad while the man she'd been talking to started barking out orders to his workers, who'd been taking a break in the corner of the plank-scattered room.

Mina seemed content, and she smiled as she perused whatever she'd brought up on her computer screen.

Chet saw the old Mina—the constant who kept him steady—and a flicker of devilment snuck up on him as he eased on over.

"Mornin'," he said over her shoulder.

He saw some pastel blocks—the kind little kids played with in a nursery—decorating the edges of the site she'd brought up on her iPad. But she flinched and hid the screen from him before he could see much more.

Eyes wide, she got that same strange look on her face that he'd seen during their walk, as if she was guilty, or as if she'd been…

Caught?

Chet wasn't sure what was what as she touched something on her computer and acted just a bit too casual for him not to notice.

"Morning to you, too," she said, gesturing toward her computer. "I was just going over details for the day care center."

There it was then. She'd been gathering decorating tips for the guests who'd be toting their children.

She frowned. "I thought we were meeting in about an hour."

"We are. I'm just wandering around, getting a feel for the place. Where're you off to next?"

"The pavilion. The crew is going to finish it up today, and I want a look-see."

"Mind if I come along?"

She nodded, noncommittal, but her smile was welcoming as they walked out of the lodge and into the clear morning air. He liked how the sun played with Mina's hair, bringing out the deep red, flirting with the gold. He only wished she didn't have it in that confining braid.

But he had no business thinking like that. He'd danced pretty close to the fire last night, bringing up her social life, finding out about her ex-boyfriend. Maybe he'd just wanted to see if the sky would fall down around them, but it hadn't.

They were getting back to where they'd been before and he couldn't be happier about it.

Walking the rock-lined path, they passed what would be a gift shop with souvenir ranch items as well as sporting and spa essentials. Then they got to the barbecue area, which was coming together with picnic tables and a stage for entertainment. Nearby stood the restaurant, where Chef Arnett's healthy gourmet food would be served, then the sports center, which would offer a full gym as well as classes like yoga, dance and fencing.

They came to the pavilion, where hikers would meet early in the morning to hit the trails in guided groups. Wood was scattered around, but the rest of the spired structure hinted of the bands that would play there, the dance floor that would sit under the sparkle of fairy lights strung down from the ceiling and through the nearby Joshua trees.

"This'll look good by the end of the day," Mina said,

a grin on her face, as if she were imagining an innocent dance with someone.

With a blast of desire, Chet realized that he hoped it was him.

But…good Lord. He wasn't in a position to be hoping anything. He'd already taken too much from her, and to think that she would suffer the ups and downs of his life while he straightened it out was just too much. He wouldn't ask that of anyone.

Yet there he was, admiring how the sun slanted down and painted half her face golden. He adored how the light freckles dusting her nose and cheekbones gave her a playful air, even when she seemed so serious and professional.

Before he could even think about what he was doing, he touched her cheek, and it felt right, just like that night.

Just like he was made to be doing it.

And when Mina turned those green eyes on him, he didn't back away.

Even if every instinct shouted that he should.

Chapter Three

Tingles shimmied down Mina's body as she reveled in the feel of Chet's fingers skimming her cheek.

This was how it should be between them—no questions about what was right and wrong, or about office propriety.

He was a man, she was a woman, and right now it was achingly clear that nothing should hold them back from wanting and needing each other.

Or from having a family together.

She sucked in a breath, so ready for him. For a moment, she even thought he was just as ready, too. That he'd forgotten about everything except the here and now, the desire that kept bringing them together.

Her lips parted, a pulse away from a whisper in which she could say, *Just kiss me. Show me that we're not only about business. Show me what's really in your heart...*

But then something in Chet's eyes changed—that all-too-familiar darkness taking over and switching the hue of his gaze from passion to wariness.

The return of the world and all its problems.

As frustration gripped Mina, she could see that he was desperate to cover up whatever he was feeling. When he grinned, then tweaked her cheek, just as if she was some kind of little sister or pal, she didn't know how to react.

Not that she needed to respond, anyway, because Chet was already backing off from her, hooking a thumb into his belt loop and nudging his hat up an inch as he surveyed the pavilion again. Just as if that's what he'd been doing all along.

"Yeah," he said in that cowboy drawl—the one that would always mark him as a rancher who'd turned tycoon rather than the other way around. "This'll do real nicely."

Mina wanted to hurl questions at him, like, *What just happened here? When are you going to stop running from not only me, but from everything?*

But…baby steps, just like last night over dinner.

Had it all been an act though? Judging by how skittish he seemed right now, they weren't on any more solid ground than before.

"So," he said, "I'll see you in an hour?"

"Okay."

Chet was already on his way, obviously having decided that it wasn't the greatest idea to be taking this walk with her. It seemed as if he was on the other side of the earth with this gaping distance between them.

Back to business, she accessed her iPad, raising her voice to catch him before he was gone. "You didn't really test anything out in the spa yet. I'm going to do that later today. Should I schedule anything for you?"

"I think the spa's best left to you. I'm not a massage-and-facial kind of guy."

And there was that grin again—the one that might've fooled her if she didn't know him so well.

As he moved down the path, she restrained a sigh, trying not to watch him in those jeans. Trying not to notice the denim clinging to his rear, his muscular thighs or even the shirt that didn't do much to hide the corded muscles of his back through the linen.

Hopeless. She was incredibly, hopelessly in love and she didn't know how to pull herself out of it. Leave it to her to fall for the most inaccessible man on earth.

But Mina had no control over her heart and what it did—not even a perfect administrative assistant could line up her emotions like a well-ordered office.

Birds warbled around her in the morning air as she took a stroll around the rest of the property, marking "done" on the checklist that she carried on her personal computer whenever she noticed progress being made. She kept looking at the time, bound and determined to get back to her cabin in the next ten minutes, in time for the Skype conversation she'd scheduled with her older sister, Katie, on the computer. Mina's niece, Lizzie, had her first preschool open house tonight, and one of the activities that her niece was going to take part in was a dance number. Mina couldn't make it, but Lizzie had begged her mom to let her show off to Mina beforehand instead.

It would be a quick chat, leaving her just enough time to meet Chet in the offices before he went to his ranch appointments.

When Mina entered the cabin, the scent of cedar welcomed her. So did the trickle of water from the rock fountain in the midst of dimly lit granite nooks and ferns in the living area.

She sat on an overstuffed leather couch, opening the notebook computer that rested on the rough-hewn coffee table. Before she logged on for two-way visual communication through the Skype camera at the top of her computer screen, Mina checked her emails.

Most were from friends, not only those she'd kept in contact with from college, but a few from San Antonio, too. She hadn't told any of them about her pregnancy, although she'd been tempted to so many times.

Soon, it was time for her video chat, and her older sister Katie called her via the computer, which rang before Mina accessed it.

A video image appeared, featuring Katie, who looked just as tidy as always with her long strawberry-blond hair held back by a headband, her green eyes sparkling.

"Mina!" she said.

Then a tinier, younger voice came over the computer. "Auntie Mina!"

A head topped by a high red ponytail—one like Pebbles Flintstone had worn back in the day—blipped into view as three-year-old Lizzie jumped up.

"Hey!" Mina laughed at the antics of her only niece. So far, there'd been no nephews, either, so Mina was addicted to everything Lizzie did and said.

"Auntie Mina, Auntie Mina!" Lizzie was climbing onto her mother's lap. "Ready to see?"

"You bet."

Lizzie preened in front of the camera, this way and that, her freckled face delighted as she modeled the pink costume she would be wearing tonight. Her mom, a whiz with a needle and thread, had whipped together a fairy-inspired outfit for her.

Mina noticed a crucial element was missing. "Don't tell me you haven't earned your wings yet."

Lizzie giggled and veered closer to the lens. "No. Mommy said later."

Katie chimed in. "I still have a little more work to do on those wings, but she'll be wearing them for the show."

The little girl had already slid off Katie's lap and, seconds later, was back with the wings, which looked like gossamer daydreams that any little girl would adore.

"See?" she said, putting them so close to the camera that they merely looked like sparkly blurs.

"Gorgeous!" Mina said nonetheless. "I just wish I could be there."

Lizzie lowered the wings from the lens, and Katie wriggled her way out from under her daughter, standing up, then taking the wings from Lizzie. Alone now, the little girl's green-blue eyes were wide and sad.

"I wish you were here."

Something stirred in Mina's chest, then in her tummy. Yearning. A keening desire for a child just as sweet as Lizzie.

Once again, the news Mina carried begged to be revealed.

Soon, Lizzie would have a cousin. Four and a half months soon. But Mina wanted to see the joy on Lizzie's face *now,* wanted the rest of her family to celebrate this miracle with her, although she wasn't so sure about their response.

Good heavens—she could just imagine how Chet

might have to undergo a bunch of questions about his family scandal and why he and Mina weren't married yet. Could just picture her conservative family wondering if she'd hooked up with another commitment-shy Michael.

"*Can't* you come tonight?" Lizzie asked Mina.

"I'm afraid not. I'm far away right now, in another state called Utah."

Lizzie nodded, but Mina was pretty sure the girl didn't know what a state was. Or Utah. But Mina would show her next time she visited, telling Lizzie more about the places she got to travel on business. Her niece loved Auntie Mina's stories.

"But," Mina said, "I aim to see you dancing around in that fairy costume sometime soon, just after I get back to Texas. Will you put on a show for me then?"

This time, Lizzie's nod was even more emphatic. "And I can dance *now* for you."

And, with that, she hopped off the chair. Mina couldn't get a full view of her, since her niece was nearly out of the camera's view, but she got the impression that Lizzie was spinning around, her arms over her head like a pixie ballerina.

Katie came to the rescue and pointed the lens toward Lizzie, who still jumped and swept out her arms all around as she previewed her show.

When she was done, Mina applauded, wishing she could give her niece a great big hug, too.

Instead, she took solace in resting her hand on her belly after she was done with the bravos.

Her own girl or boy. She hadn't wanted to know the sex during her first ultrasound. Didn't want to know until she told Chet.

Or could it be that she'd put off the discovery because the news of the pregnancy hadn't seemed real during her visit to the doctor?

Now, though, it was getting more real by the day, and tears needled the back of Mina's eyes as she felt more alone than ever in this.

When a knock sounded on her front door, she prayed that her sorrow wasn't obvious.

Through the glass that decorated the thick door, she saw a hint of cowboy: jeans, boots, hat.

Chet?

"Come in!" she shouted. Then she turned to the computer. "Lizzie, you're going to be wonderful tonight. Big kisses. I love you!"

"Love you!" Lizzie blew kisses at the screen and flitted off.

Mina heard the door shut, then boot steps. She glanced over her shoulder to see her boss, his hat in one hand, leaving his dark blond hair ruffled.

It was as if the earth sloped, just like one of those walking ramps on a fun house that tried to throw you off balance. The irony was that Mina hadn't been having all that much fun lately.

Katie came back on, taking the camera over just in time to spy him, too. With a saucy, curious expression written all over her face, she said, "Doing business out of the office today, sis?"

Mina shot a don't-get-any-ideas glare at her sibling. It was obvious that Katie was trying to get an even better gander at Chet.

Great.

But whether things worked out with him or not, he was always going to be a part of Mina's life. Maybe they wouldn't end up married—God, Mina hoped *that* wasn't true—but he was her child's father, no buts about it.

Mina sighed. It was time to take baby steps with her family, too, introducing them to the father of her child, no matter how they might receive him.

"I'm meeting with my boss," Mina said, swiveling her computer so it would fully capture Chet on the screen. "Say hi," she said to him.

"Hi." He lifted a baffled brow at the sight of Katie on the computer.

Without any more ado, Mina turned the camera back on her. That's all Katie would get for now.

"Have fun at that open house tonight," Mina said, making it clear that Katie needed to keep any more comments to herself.

Her sister had the sort of perceptive look on her face that told Mina she suspected something was being kept from her. Mina was just too jumpy not to arouse suspicion. Heck, her own expression—lovestruck and dumb, no doubt—probably gave her away full force.

"We'll talk later?" her sister said.

Mina ignored her. "Love ya! Bye!"

And she signed off.

Before she could ask why Chet was here instead of the offices, he said, "I was antsy to get on with those ranch appointments, so here I am. Someone in administration said that they'd seen you go to your cabin. Hope you don't mind."

"Not at all." As efficient as always, she held out her hand for some papers that Chet was carrying.

But her heart was still beating from his entrance, as well as the gander Katie had gotten at the father of Mina's child.

"You know," she said, "you didn't have to print these memos out in hard copy. There're these newfangled things called computers that hold all this information."

He chuckled and took a seat in a chair next to the couch. "I don't like to stare at a screen all day."

"Right. You're an old-fashioned manly man." Her heart was beating so loudly that it overwhelmed the splash of the fountain.

She liked how old-fashioned Chet was—he was the type who would be all about slow walks through the country, slow summer nights as the crickets chirped, a slow hand…

He had found her iPad on the coffee table. "I'm not sure how my life would be much improved with all the doodads you carry around."

"Someone in your office has to be comfortable with the digital age."

"Better you than me."

Somehow, he managed to turn the "doodad" on. Mina didn't mind. He was already in her cabin, her personal space, and what she kept on her computer screens wasn't nearly as intimate.

But she changed her mind when he pressed a particular icon.

"Well, look here," he said, holding up the screen so she could see what he'd found.

It was her photo file, and it was showing a picture she'd taken about a year ago, soon after the breakup with Michael. She'd decided to take some vacation time—a rare occurrence—and go on a trip to clear her mind. She'd ended up in Savannah, Georgia, with her sister Amy, who wasn't just six years younger, she also looked more like their dark-haired dad than either Katie or Mina, the daughters who took after their redheaded mom.

This photo presented Amy, who'd been engaged to get married at the time, mugging on a park bench in one of the town squares.

"That's my baby sis on the Forrest Gump bench," Mina said. "They filmed some of the movie there in Savannah."

Chet lingered on the picture for only a moment, seeming just as unimpressed with the Hollywood trivia as he was with the doodad.

Mina tossed him a smart-aleck grin. "I don't have pictures of cattle drives or Montana wildlife on there, so I'm not sure there's much for you to get excited about."

Nonetheless, he was going from one picture to the next. And, wouldn't you know it—he stopped on a photo that Mina had meant to delete a while ago.

It was an image of him. A reflective moment she'd captured with her phone when he hadn't been aware of it. Before the scandal had hit and before all his family's skeletons had tumbled out of the closet.

He was leaning back in his office chair, one booted ankle propped on his knee as he gazed out his wide office window at the dusk-awakened lights of San Antonio. He'd almost seemed excited about his new life, the chances he might have to get to know the father who'd called him down from Montana so they might mend their fences.

Now, Chet turned off the computer screen as if he could turn off the memory of those days, too—the times when he'd been unprotected from a truth that had beaten him down not long afterward.

After the screen had gone dark, Mina swallowed hard, thinking that he might stay just as blank.

Just as tough to read and connect to as ever.

Hours later, Mina was still unsettled by her meeting with Chet. But, like most women who appreciated a good resort, she was hoping that some spa time might ease her mind.

Currently, she was wallowing in one of the thick, white terry cloth robes the facility provided as she navigated the circular indoor path that branched off into the private massage rooms. The hallway was dim, lit only by stone lanterns, with soothing music piped in through hidden speakers.

So far, she'd steered clear of the many massages on the menu—the tempting "desert rain shower" or hot stone or aromatherapy treatments. Mina had claimed to be too busy with tomorrow night's local event and had asked the rest of her staff to report their own experiences to her because, although she knew that pregnant women could get massages, she didn't want to tell a masseuse about her condition before Chet—or any of her friends and family—knew.

It just seemed wrong.

Instead, she'd decided to concentrate on the facials that the spa offered, today choosing one that used pearl powder to lend "luster to the skin," as the menu had said.

It'd done the trick, all right, and she was relaxed as she entered the Paradise Room, an area with a rock pool, a waterfall and a seductive, serene air so she could wind down before going back to work.

But, with a smile, she told herself that this *was* her work.

Best job in the world.

Water played against the pool's surface as it splashed from the rocks above. Mina took off the robe, tossing it over a nearby deck chair. She was wearing a one-piece suit that she'd plucked from the resort's gift shop stock—a modest light blue number that flattered and clung to her still basically normal curves.

Then she gave in to the lure of the room, breathing in the fresh, orange-blossom aroma.

Paradise.

But there was always a catch to it, and when she heard her phone go "ding," she knew she'd gotten a text message to interrupt her.

Since she was on the clock, she had to look.

But it was just from Mom. Then again, Mina had been expecting this after her chat with Katie.

A little birdy tells me you had a cowboy in your cabin. :)

Good heavens, it hadn't taken that long for the little birdy to spread the news. Thank goodness Mina had already decided it was permissible to let her family in on what was going on just as gradually as she was doing for Chet.

She texted back.

Don't get excited, Mom.

Her mother, who had fingers faster than any texting teen, came back with,

Well, if it was someone to get excited about, you know that he'd always be welcome for dinner.

Mina shook her head, laughing a little.

I'll keep that in mind.
Love and kisses.

And she put the phone away, absently brushing her tummy at the same time. Even if they overstepped at times, her baby was going to have a family who loved him or her. Her mom and dad would help in any way they could, if worse came to worse and she lacked for anything as a single mom.

But she wouldn't. Mina had to have faith in Chet… and in herself if things didn't work out with him. She wasn't naive enough to con herself into thinking single parenthood would be easy, but she would be prepared, just in case.

She slipped into the cool pool, sighing, letting the murmur of water make its hushed way into the very core of her. Going under the surface, she came back up again, steeped, cleansed.

Climbing out, she sat on the ledge, kicking her feet and listening to the Native American flute playing on the hidden speakers.

She smiled. This spa was going to be a big success for Chet, and she was content to be a part of what would heal him. But was that all it would take to make him whole again—the triumph of a project that was dear to his heart and pride?

When she heard someone else in the room, she stood to get a towel or her robe. But too late.

There he was—Chet. And he'd stopped in his tracks at the sight of her.

Instinctively, she rested her arm over her belly, hoping she could still hide her secret.

Just for a little while longer.

Chet felt as if the breath had been slammed out of him.

Mina...

Legs that seemed to go on forever, slim hips, breasts that cried out to be palmed by his hands.

Was she curvier than he remembered?

No. Yes. He wasn't sure. He'd tried so hard to put her out of his mind that, right now, just by looking at her, his head was a mess, not settling on anything except for how much he craved her.

She snatched a robe off of a nearby chair, but it did nothing to douse the fire that was racing through him at lightning speed.

To feel her again. To be inside of her...

"I didn't think you were coming to the spa," she said breathlessly.

He had to clear his throat, because there was something lodged in it.

"I changed my mind. After being out in the sun all day, I thought a dip in a pool would be just the thing. You talked about this Paradise Room, so..." Damn it, his voice still sounded rough.

Out of gentlemanly instinct, he'd finally looked away,

knowing from the flush on her face that she was embarrassed to have been caught like this.

But they'd been intimate, and neither of them could pretend otherwise.

When he looked back up at her, she had that robe closed, the sash tied. Yet, even though she was dressed, she seemed so painfully vulnerable.

In the face of that, *his* walls went up. He hated what he'd done to her that night, hated that he'd caused this kind of tension between them.

Even so, he wondered what it might be like if his defenses ever stayed down. But what would he be left with if not for those walls?

She began to walk out of the room. "I've got a lot to do."

"Wait, Mina."

She halted, her posture stiff, as if she expected to be called out for something.

"Don't let me chase you away," he said. And he wanted her to stay, more than anything, because when she wasn't near him, he was wishing for it.

Then again, asking her to stay wasn't going to get them back to where they'd been before he'd touched her, made love to her. Even more importantly, being alone in a seductive room while she was half-naked under that robe wasn't going to go over too well in a conservative company like the Barron Group if a staff member came in and picked up on this sexual awareness between them.

Chet wasn't worried about his reputation so much as hers, because, if the rumors started up, even his most minor fears might come true and she might never be taken seriously again.

And Chet knew the power of words. The power of a lie.

But he also knew he was lying to himself right now, making up excuses about why they shouldn't be here, standing with a curtain of anticipation between them.

She was watching him again, with that weighted look he'd noticed last night, as if she was trying to figure what was running through his mind.

"You have no idea what to do with yourself, do you, Chet?"

Once again, she could see right through him.

"Things were so simple eight months ago," he said. "I'm trying to figure out why they can't be that way now."

"Things change."

Hearing her say it drove this new reality home. Things *had* changed, and he was sure doing a poor job of rolling with it.

That shamed him somewhat, because he'd always believed himself to be a stronger man than that. And what he was seeing in himself wasn't acceptable: this wasn't the person Abe had raised from boyhood up before they'd gone their own ways.

Was this *Eli* coming out in him?

Mina waited there in her robe, as if she was still wishing that he would say more.

But he couldn't and when she walked away, she took a little bit of his hopes with her, leaving him as aimless as ever.

Chapter Four

That evening after dinner, Chet's entire staff met at the pavilion, where they were having a "game night," just like the ones that would be offered to the guests once the resort opened. A few of the local contractors had shown up, too.

There was an excited buzz in the air, everyone getting to know each other outside of work as Danny, one of the young Barron Group staffers, stood next to Mina, his hands stuffed into his khaki pants pockets. Meanwhile, another staffer, Corrine, who'd put together tonight's activity, welcomed everyone.

Danny leaned over to Mina and whispered, "I'm gonna make sure I'm on your side." They were going to play a round of softball—a team-building exercise. "I figure backing up the boss might score me some points."

As Danny shot her a grin, she realized that he

wasn't talking about Chet—he was referring to *her* as the boss.

A glow of pride caught her right in the middle of the chest. This resort development had been the first big project that Chet had let her run with, but she'd never looked at herself as anything more than his assistant.

Yet, what would Danny and the others think if they knew that Chet had given Mina more responsibilities at this resort *after* they'd been together?

She tried not to believe that Chet had raised her status out of guilt or favoritism. Chet had gradually been giving her other projects with higher esteem for a while now, even before that night. Besides, he was a fair man in general, and when he said that he wanted to make sure that no one thought she had slept her way to the top, he'd meant it.

But maybe he was right about what might happen if the staff knew—they might not look at her the same way ever again. That's why it was imperative that, when she told Chet about the baby, it would be because she was more than just a one-night stand or the mother of his child.

It would be because he loved her.

Nobody would have any doubts about what she meant to him.

As Corrine led the group toward a field lined by rough bleachers, a chain-link backstop and lights that buttered the ground with illumination, Mina was determined to have some fun, to not think about anything else for a couple of hours.

But it was hard when all she was doing was glancing around for Chet, who hadn't shown up yet.

She sought a position in left field since she'd never

been a softball kind of girl. Danny, who'd indeed ended up on her team, stood next to her.

As he loitered with his arms crossed over the logo of his long-sleeved T-shirt—an ad for surfboards—Mina could tell that he was probably more into watching sports on TV than actually playing.

Their pitcher was lobbing high, slow balls at Corrine, the first up at the plate.

"Hey, batter batter," Danny said, almost as if he was poking fun at this entire exercise. Then, already bored, he turned to Mina. "If I didn't know any better, I'd say you almost look like one of *us* tonight."

"Us?" Mina peered down at her game-night garb. Roomy jeans, sneakers, an untucked blouse.

"I'm talking about someone who's just starting to climb the corporate ladder," Danny said. "*My* kind of person."

"I am your kind of person. I'm just a little further up the ladder." Mina smiled. "I've done my share of climbing over the years."

"You're lucky that you got assigned to Chet Barron. He's been a real good mentor for you."

Was Danny getting around to what she was afraid he was getting around to? Was it obvious that she and Chet had…hit it off?

"In business," she said, "you make your own luck, Danny. The rest is work."

"I know, and you've got a reputation as a hard worker. People around here like you, Mina. They're happy to see your fortunes rising."

Just when she was getting ready for him to deliver the zinger, Danny sent her a crooked grin.

And she realized what was really going on.

He was making small talk. Flirting?

Good heavens. Danny wasn't even out of his early twenties. Was he making his own luck, as he'd put it, searching for his own mentor?

There was a popping sound from the batter's box, and they both set their attention on the fly ball traveling toward first base.

As one of the contractors fielded it, Mina glanced around again, this time spying Chet near the bleachers, where he was leaning, arms casually crossed over his chest, his cowboy hat low over his brow.

A shock jolted her, in her chest and then lower, tightening.

Something wicked in Mina wondered if he'd seen Danny cozying up to her, if she should play this out just to get a reaction out of Chet—to determine if he cared. Or if he was jealous.

But she just didn't have the heart to test him that way, especially when Chet glanced away from her as if he knew Mina had seen him looking.

The shortstop called out to Danny, pointing toward the empty center field.

"I think that guy is serious about his game," Mina said. "Better get on over there."

Danny laughed. "Yes, boss."

And he wandered off toward center field. But he didn't stop there. He ended up in right field, where Chef Arnett's cute sous chef was positioned.

Mina peered back to where Chet had been lingering, only to find that he'd already left.

Did he care?

Her veins filled with rushing hope as she promised herself that she was going to find out soon, once and for all.

Chet had no right to be jealous.

None at all.

And he kept telling himself this after he settled back into his makeshift office, the halls empty, the lights shaded as the cleaning crew made their rounds.

It would've been nice to relax with the staff, letting off some steam out there, but the sight of Mina in left field with that young pup Danny Hogan, a known flirt, had stopped Chet cold.

He wasn't used to seeing Mina with anyone else but him. Wasn't used to seeing her in casual clothes, talking with other men, especially ones who were still young and untouched enough by the trials of life to have charming, carefree smiles.

Sure, Mina needed some levity in her life, but Chet was sure someone like Danny Hogan was too flighty for her needs, especially after what she'd told him about that ex-boyfriend of hers.

If Chet saw Danny making a play for Mina again, he'd…

What—shoo the kid off?

Or…

Damn, there was something else going on here—something Chet could barely admit. He was acting as if Mina had been getting ready to betray him, just as his own mom had betrayed Abe.

Chet leaned back in his leather chair, raking a hand through his hair. What did he expect—for Mina to become a nun after their one night together, after he'd made it perfectly clear that they didn't have a romantic future?

As he'd done before when life seemed to be piling up on him, he turned his attention to work. He worked until night covered the sky, until he knew that the softball game had to be over and Mina was back in her cabin.

Trying not to think about how much he hoped she was alone, Chet went back to his own cabin but had a hell of a time getting to sleep.

Fortunately, in the morning he was busy while the staff charged around, getting ready for the locals preview day that they were holding so that they could start establishing a reputation in the community. Hopefully, the resort could whip up some early enthusiasm and end up establishing regular customers besides their visiting clientele.

When Chet emerged from his cabin after an on-the-fly breakfast from his cabin kitchen, he found the property bustling with the staff setting up their tents and tables and a local band bringing their equipment to the pavilion. The resort's restaurant crew was preparing an area that would feature their food while, nearby, the spa and activities staff would be offering mini-massages, product samples and short hikes on the fringes of the common area, now that the weather was cooling off near the end of the day.

Somehow, he and Mina didn't see each other the whole time, although Chet heard her voice over the walkie-talkies that the staff carried. And every time he did, his blood caught on fire, heating him to distraction.

When he finally saw Mina, it was early evening in the food area, where a bunch of linen-covered tables boasted samples from the restaurant. There was already a casually dressed crowd, sipping wine, enjoying themselves.

Mina was schmoozing with some local politicians and businessmen, and she looked so fresh and beautiful in her prairie skirt, boots and white peasant top that she took Chet's breath away, leaving him standing there like a dolt.

When was he going to get over this?

Knowing he would have to start the process, he went over to join her group.

She saw him before he even arrived, and he recognized the same posture he'd spied in her last night, when she'd been in left field and he'd been standing by the bleachers.

Widened eyes. The obvious flare of attraction in her gaze.

She had to feel the same way he did, and it scared him to death, because he didn't know what the hell to do about it.

"Chet," Mina said when he arrived on the fringes of her social circle. She'd recovered nicely from their moment, going on to introduce everyone.

He shook hands all around, knowing that he would be wining and dining these people before he left to check on other Group projects later tomorrow; in fact, he would be having a lunch with several locals before going to the airport.

"Thanks for coming," he said to them. "Is there anything I can get for anyone?"

The mayor, a man with a handlebar mustache and a certain Wild West air, held up his glass of red wine. "I think you've provided nicely, Mr. Barron."

"Chet. It's Chet."

He and Mina traded a smile, and it had the power to let him know that things were going to be okay, that this resort was going to flourish.

But the crackling awareness between them didn't go anywhere.

He made it through the rest of the night, remembering her smile, remembering the way Mina's skirt fell over her hips, the way her hair rested on her shoulders and caught the last of the sun as it set.

In the end, when the visitors had left and the area was cleaned up, he found her on a bench in front of the administration building, exhausted, her skirt spread around her, her eyes closed.

A beat of concern seized his heart, but when she seemed to sense him, then opened her eyes and grinned, he knew that she was undergoing a good kind of exhaustion. The kind he'd grown used to over the years, after a decent day's work that bolstered the spirit.

"We did it," she said.

Chet pushed back the brim of his hat. "*You* did it. I just looked over your plans and gave my okay, that's all."

"You put your everything into this place. Give yourself some credit."

She was rubbing her arms, and for the first time tonight, he noticed a coolness in the air. Fall was definitely descending in the desert, and fast.

"Tonight might be a good time for a fire," he said. "What do you say I light up that pit on my cabin deck while we debrief?"

"I vote yes."

He held out his hand to her and she grabbed on to it,

just as she had the other night when they'd tested Chef Arnett's cooking.

The same jarring electricity traveled through him as he brought her to her feet. When he let go, they started to walk on the graveled path to his cabin, and he could've sworn that she was just as puzzled about what to say now as he was.

On the way, Chet saw Danny Hogan and that sous chef he'd been chatting up at the softball game in the near distance, walking over a hill.

"The spirit path," Mina said. "I'll bet he's taking her there."

"For some kind of deep religious experience?"

Mina gave him a little punch to the arm. "Nice."

"What?" It was easy to be in a good mood, knowing that Danny Hogan had decided to pursue a girl who wasn't named Mina. "The kid's known around the office for loving his entertainment."

"Kid? Listen to you, like you're such an ancient creature."

Who knew that thirty would *feel* so old? It was as if Chet had lived a lot of lifetime from birth to the present. But with the moon and stars shining down like they were, and with Mina walking right next to him, things seemed new right now.

He wished it would stay that way—that they could be locked in this moment under the stars, where he didn't ever have to go back to what he'd been running from.

"Are you looking forward to Jeremiah's wedding?" she asked, changing the subject.

He took a breath, let it out. "Yeah, for my brother's sake. Jeremiah's crazy about Ally, and I'm happy for him. It's just that Eli might be there, if he's earned any time out of rehab."

"Maybe you can avoid him."

Chet recalled how shamed he'd felt just yesterday, when he'd realized that it was high time that he faced his demons.

"No," he said. "There's no more avoiding what I need to confront."

Saying it felt right, as if he'd relieved himself of a burden he hadn't known how to release.

Mina paused, the moonlight brushing over her. She looked at him, the corners of her mouth turned up, her eyes shining.

"I'm glad to hear that, Chet."

"I'm glad I finally feel that way." Then he shrugged. "In any case, I've got two brothers waiting for me in Texas. And they've been waiting for a while. After Eli screwed up for the last time, we knew we'd have to figure out how to handle him beyond rehab."

"Just let me know what I can do. Promise you'll do that and not take all of this on yourself. You're not alone, Chet."

"I know."

He would never be alone—not with Mina around.

How could he have forgotten that she was the first one he'd turned to in his crisis? That she had never let him down, even when he'd done it to her?

He was talking before he knew it. "Did you get the wedding invitation for Jeremiah and Ally?"

"Yes."

She didn't add more. She didn't have to because, even though she'd attended Tyler's wedding as a business acquaintance, it'd been awkward. Maybe she'd been thinking about staying away from *this* Barron event, intent on avoiding more emotional clumsiness with Chet.

He talked before he even realized something had come out of his mouth. "Maybe we can go together."

"To...the wedding?"

Had he just asked her out?

He tried to recover. "It was just an idea. I figure we'll both be traveling at the same time, from San Antonio to the ranch, and it made sense for us to just do it together."

"Oh." Her voice was so soft, so vulnerable, that it nearly killed him.

Now look what he'd done—caused another weird situation.

He tried again. "Besides traveling together, I'd actually like to be around you there."

"You...would?"

"Yes." And he meant it.

With that one word—*yes*—he'd jumped off a mountain without anything to catch him below. Nothing but Mina.

They'd both slowed to a stand on the path.

"Weddings," she said. "They can be so boring unless you've got someone to talk to the whole time."

"Or to watch all the rituals with—like the bride and groom eating the first slice of cake."

"Or seeing everyone dancing to all the bad music."

Was she waiting for him to claim a spot on her dance card now?

Hell, he would love a dance with her—a slow one, where he could just hold her and sway to the music.

A worm of reality wiggled into his thoughts. Was

she what he really needed, or was he going to end up sucking her all the way into his problems, taking her down with him?

Goose bumps paraded over her arms, and he wasn't sure if they were from the cooling night or from this conversation that was fast swerving out of control.

"Damn it, you're probably freezing out here," he said, seizing the chance to save himself with another change of topic.

"I'm fine."

As he started down the path to his cabin again, she reached out, gripping his arm.

"I'm *fine,* Chet."

Did she mean more than just that though? Was she telling him that, if he stepped out of this self-imposed shell, if he were to seize the day and take up where their one beautiful night together had left off, she could handle it? That if he were to scoop her into his arms and sweep her the rest of the short way down this path and into his cabin, she might even welcome it?

Trouble was, he wasn't sure what would come after all that.

Or if *he* could handle it.

It was times like these, when Chet was being so darned wooden in the head, that Mina thought that she might have to start looking for a new job.

If she did, she might never have to let him know about their child. She could go off to a place where no one knew her, where they wouldn't care about who the father of her baby was, then start anew. That way, Chet could concentrate on his decimated life and not worry about anything else.

But, far below the surface, questions jabbed at Mina. Was there a chance that a child could mend Chet's fractured soul?

Couldn't *she* do that for him, too?

Believing in the possibility with every fiber of her being, she took the biggest risk ever.

Heart ramming against her chest, she lifted up to her tiptoes, pushing back Chet's cowboy hat, closing her eyes, tentatively touching her lips to his.

Paradise. As sensual as the sound of water falling. As perfect as any haven she could imagine.

It was as if something broke open in him, and he slipped his arms around her, holding her close as heaven swirled through her, as they sipped at each other, warm and lingering.

Chet.

Their second kiss, but this one was so much more wonderful than the first one, when he'd needed more than just her.

She breathed, pulled back a little, whispering against him. "You bet I'll go to that wedding with you."

I'll go anywhere, if you'd just ask.

But *he* had to be the one to bring up that he wanted more. He had to be obvious about wanting her, showing her without any outside influence that he had come to terms with his life and that there was room enough for her, plus one.

She'd obviously hit a button in him, and he guided them off the path, toward a large pine that spread its branches and blocked out the sky.

Privacy, she thought. He didn't want anyone to see.

Gently, he leaned her against the pine, cupping the

back of her head with a hand, tilting her face up to him just before he covered her mouth with his again.

And, just like that, she was in another place. A glass ball where nothing else mattered, just them, just this moment, an endless stretch of warmth and vibration that shimmered down her body.

Over her skin.

Under it.

Every inch of her was going liquid, hot and wanting.

She slid her palms up his back, feeling every muscle that had survived his time behind a desk, muscles that had been created by hard work on his ranch—riding, roping, straining under the sun as sweat dappled his skin.

Wanting to feel him all the way against her, she deepened the kiss, pulling him down, opening her mouth, nearly devouring him in her wild need. She was going tight all over—her breasts, the center of her—and she was going to need a release.

Him—her ultimate release.

She panted, "I've been wishing this would happen for so long. You don't know what it's been like, waiting for you, hoping…"

"I know," he said raggedly, his fingers threaded through her hair.

He knew.

He'd thought about kissing her again, too, holding her, pressing her against his body so that she could feel just how *much* he'd been wishing for her.

She pulled his hat off his head, clutching it as he came down for another kiss, just as hungry for her as she was for him.

This time he wasn't kissing her with the desperation of a grieving man, a man who was searching for a truth. Now, he took it slow, sliding his tongue past her lips, exploring as she melted beneath him, so overwhelmed that he had to hold her up when her knees gave out.

Her breasts were aching for a touch, more sensitive than she'd ever known because of the pregnancy but especially now, as he brushed a hand over one, tenderly....

Almost lovingly.

But Mina wouldn't believe that. Not until she *heard* him say it.

"Chet," she said on a near moan.

Encouraged, he circled her nipple with a thumb. With the lace of her bra and her blouse between her and his skin, all she wanted to do was strip off her clothing, be with him entirely.

She reached up, undoing one button, then another. If this went where she hoped it would go, she would be careful with him, be careful of the baby...

Nearby an owl hooted, reminding her that they weren't alone.

"Not here," he said, his breath warm against her ear, sending more sizzles through her.

"Your cabin?" she asked.

When he paused, she knew that this was a make-or-break moment.

Somewhere along the way, she'd dropped his hat, so she used both hands to cup his head, making him look right at her.

"You make me so happy," she said.

His gaze was unfocused, desire-ridden. "I do?"

"You always have."

And she brought him down for another kiss, no matter where they were, no matter who might come upon them out here in the open.

He held her, clearly unable to stop, and Mina wanted so badly to call it love.

Just thinking about it, she lost her balance again, and he caught her, then lifted her into his arms, taking her the rest of the way to his cabin.

Chapter Five

Chet crashed through his cabin door, holding Mina, kissing her.

You make me so happy, she'd said.

And she'd meant it in a way that went beyond anything he'd ever had with *anyone* before.

That should've scared the life out of him, but how could it when he knew that here, with her in his arms, she really was everything he needed and he'd just been too afraid to admit it?

Her face was nuzzled against his neck while she held tight to him, her breath like the tiny beat of butterfly wings against his throat. The fluttering sensation echoed inside of him, except a hundred times faster.

When he got to the staircase that led to his loft bedroom, he eased her down until she stood on the first step, bringing them nearly face-to-face.

She leaned toward him, feverish, running her fingers

through his hair. He remembered that his hat was somewhere outside, on the ground, but he didn't really care.

"Mina," he whispered, cradling her jaw with one hand, wanting to map every nuance of her face. First her cheekbones, curved and high, a work of art. Then her mouth.

She kissed the tip of his thumb. "This time, I want to wake up and see you in the morning, next to me."

The last time had been a maelstrom of feeling and urgency, and he wanted more between them, too. Wanted it to last all night long.

He answered her by coasting his fingers down her neck, her collarbone. She gasped, leaning back her head, exposing the white of her throat in the near darkness. He could barely see her, but he knew her through and through, just by touch, by his desire and affection for her.

Affection, he thought while dragging his fingers lower, down, between her breasts. He didn't know if he would ever be able to love anyone—trust was a part of love and he just didn't have that in him anymore—but he would come closest to it with Mina.

He would give her everything but that deep, dark place inside of him that he would have to protect from pain, because he didn't think he could take even an iota more of it.

She shivered as he traveled down the center of her upper stomach, but when he got to her belly, she grasped his wrist.

"Here," she whispered, leading him back up to her breast.

His hand opened over its fullness. Damn it, before

tonight, he'd forgotten how glorious it was to feel a woman. Feel Mina.

He braced one hand over her back, spread the other one over her breast, then used his fingertips to trace her nipple, which pebbled against her bra and blouse. Bending to her, he kissed her there, feeling the hard nub, rubbing his lips over it until she moaned.

A blast of heat made him realize that he was already hard, straining against his jeans. He used his tongue to lave her nipple, dampening her blouse, making her clutch at his shoulders.

Her breathing had turned to panting, his blood to a rush of molten lava, urging him on.

He pushed up her shirt, and he lowered himself, pressing his lips to her upper stomach. She inhaled harshly.

"Wait," she said.

Then she was undoing the rest of her buttons, practically ripping off her blouse. He helped her, pushing off the material, leaving her in a lace bra that he could see in the night-shrouded room.

She made quick work of that, too, dropping it to the ground.

Seeing the blush of her nipples against the pale of her skin was too much for him, and he cupped both of her breasts. They were beautiful, plump and round. Perfect.

He put his attention on the one that he hadn't kissed earlier, taking her nipple into his mouth, sucking, loving it while she whimpered.

Her little sounds drove him crazy, and he wrapped her in his arms, lifting her gently, bringing her to the top of the stairway to his bed—a span of pale quilt and mattress that welcomed them as he lay her down on it.

Moonlight spilled through the circular window above, casting silver light over the part of Mina that was caught by its illumination. Her smiling face, her hair, a spill of red on the white of the quilt. Her breasts, ripe and gorgeous. Her arms reaching out for him.

He wrestled off his shirt, his boots and socks, then crawled onto the bed, poised over her as she gripped his forearms.

"I tried to put you out of my mind," he said, his voice gritty. "But you stayed there."

"You stayed with me, too."

He slid an arm under her, then lowered himself until his chest came down on hers. Her breasts crushed against him, and he almost died, right there and then, stimulated beyond belief, flesh to flesh.

He kissed her again, deeply, thoroughly, slow, agonizing. His tongue explored her mouth with long, languorous strokes.

All night long.

The mere thought sent a deluge of warmth through him, down every limb, coating him, animating him for the first time in what seemed like forever.

He wanted to know more of her than he'd ever gotten to before, wanted to claim every inch of skin, every curve.

When he came up for air, he smoothed his hand over a breast again—damn, he couldn't get enough of them—then her waist. He felt her belt, the skirt beneath it.

Mina shifted underneath him, using her fingers to gradually hike up her skirt.

He took the hint and skimmed his fingers under the material and over her thigh, playing there, lightly tracing, making her squirm.

He smiled. It was so easy with her. So easy to be satisfied because he made her happy. He couldn't believe that he had the ability to draw such feeling from her.

When he coasted his fingertips between her legs, she gasped.

"Yes. There…" she whispered.

She parted her legs for him, and he tugged down her panties enough to slip his fingers inside the lace material.

She was ready for him.

Already ready.

And he was, too, pounding, throbbing for her. Nearly to the bursting point.

It wasn't time yet, though. Not nearly time.

As he slid a finger between her folds, she arched. And when he found the most sensitive part of her, she cried out.

He concentrated there, watching her moonlight-revealed face—every time she bit her lip, every time she opened her mouth to make another soft sound…

When he coaxed a finger all the way inside of her, she grabbed at his arm again, digging into his skin.

He barely felt it as her breathing escalated, heavier, faster.…

Moans.

Groans—

She cried out again, rocking her hips, saying his name.

He watched every moment, all twisted up inside, needing a release, too.

After she reached her peak, then relaxed on the bed, she didn't stay still for long, seeking the fly of his jeans.

"I've got it," he said, rising from the bed, standing and shucking off the denim. Then he removed her boots, her skirt, her panties, leaving her bare to him.

He could still only see from the waist up in that circle of moonlight and, when she spoke, he watched her mouth.

That gorgeous, full mouth.

"I want you so much."

It didn't take but a minute to go to his shaving kit for protection, then free the condom from its packet and put it on. He came to the bed again, lying down next to her, and she shifted so that she was facing him, side to side.

Without a word, just their breathing, just the night sounds outside the cabin, he rested his hand on her hip.

She didn't say anything, either. Then again, she didn't need to. He could see every thought written over her face.

Her affection for him.

And maybe even *more* than that?

His pulse jogged even faster as she pulled him close, wrapping one of her legs over him until his hardness nudged her.

"I'm so happy," she whispered again.

He was, too, but the words stuck in his throat. He was happier than he'd ever been.

Unable to stand it any longer, he eased into her, moving with a nice, slow rhythm so he could enjoy every pulsating instant.

She was with him all the way, pressing close, her lips against his throat.

"Chet," she said, and he loved to hear it, because

when it came from her, he had no doubt about who he was. She knew how to define him even when he couldn't do so.

The cadence of their lovemaking got faster, more demanding. Each moment nailed his heart, and it nearly beat out of his chest, taking over the rest of his body as it thudded hard.

Harder.

It was as if something was pounding at him, pulling him this way, that way, turning him upside down, in and out—

Finally, he did burst, and it felt as if he'd blasted right open, revealing everything about himself to her.

Afterward, as he held her close, he wondered if it was because he was overcome by emotion or if it was because he didn't want her to see the look on his face.

The complete and utter decimation of a man who would have to piece himself back together again come tomorrow, when he would have to go back to real life.

After they'd snuggled a bit, Chet left the bed, giving Mina a chance to slip under the covers.

She was glad that she wasn't obviously pregnant to the casual eye, otherwise she would've been cautious about having him touch or see her belly. The biggest change she'd undergone so far was her breasts, which had become so sensitized that even a brush of his fingertips had sent a blast crashing through her.

As she thought about how he'd responded to *her,* all fire and passion, she hugged a pillow to her chest. He'd lived up to every fantasy.

But what came next was all reality.

Was now a good time to tell him?

The most defensive part of her screamed "No!" It was still too early. Even though she'd hoped this would change everything between them, making love again hadn't done that. It hadn't meant his issues had disappeared and everything would be hunky-dory now.

And it didn't erase her concerns, either.

Her heart was blipping. Nerves.

Now, more than ever, Mina *needed* to hear him say, "I love you." She had to have a commitment. Maybe she could blame it on her last relationship, when she hadn't gotten anything close to promises or vows.

This time, she wanted to know that the man she'd chosen was with her because he couldn't imagine life any other way. And that's why she didn't say a word about the baby, even though she knew there would come a time when she would *have* to tell Chet, love or not.

But, after what had just happened between them, she was sure Chet was going to tell her he loved her. Maybe not tonight, but someday soon.

As he came back to the bed, she sighed. Looking at him always did that to her.

He had some height as well as heft, all muscle, as solid as they came. Feeling him against her had made her think that no other man would ever come close to doing what Chet did to her.

There would *never* be another like him, and that's the way it should be, too. The father of her child should be the end-all and be-all.

He lifted the covers, going under them, as well. A puff of air whisked over Mina, releasing goose bumps all over her body—especially when she caught scent of his skin.

Musky, manly, with a hint of sweet clover and hay.

"Hey, cowboy," she said softly.

He paused, as if thinking something over. Then he pulled her to him, bringing her back to his chest as he cradled her.

Heart banging with this show of affection, Mina hugged his arms against her chest, closing her eyes, her throat clogged.

Yes, someday he was going to tell her he loved her.

"I was thinking," he said, "that we should've tried to see more of the sights around here before we had to go."

Joy zipped through her. He was hinting that he regretted not being with her more outside of this bedroom.

"There're a lot of things to see around St. George," she said, encouraging him.

"Yeah," he said. "Zion Park's pretty close by. Maybe next time we're here, we can drive up there."

Mina was normally a pretty active gal, and under different circumstances she would've loved the type of challenging hikes Mt. Zion could offer. But she couldn't push herself physically in her state.

"I'd like Zion," she said. "But only if we'd do a wimpy hike or just…I don't know, strolled around."

"Since when are you a wimp? Weren't you the one who tried skydiving when we went to San Diego in April to check out that hotel property?"

"Yes, that was me. And I've never recovered." Actually, being a daredevil for the first time in her life had been loads of fun, but it wasn't something she would ever do again. "My heart barely survived the first time."

"All right then. We could go wimpy but, understand, you'd kill my male ego."

She nuzzled the crook of his arm. "We can build it back up again pretty quick, you know."

"You'll have to give me a minute on that," he said.

Then he laughed, and the vibrations carried through from his chest into her back. It was just more proof of a connection between them, a wire that ran between him and her.

She smiled into his skin, loving the smell of him. She'd read once that scent had a lot to do with attraction, and Chet did it for her. He was an addiction.

"The other night," she said, "you were talking about how I should take a real vacation. But what about you?"

She wanted to know where he would like to go, what he would love to do.

Who he would do it with.

"Vacation," he said. "I'm not sure I'll ever get one."

"You're that much of a workaholic?" Like his brother Tyler once was before he'd found his new wife, Zoe.

"I'm sure as hell turning into an office hound."

"But you won't be that way forever."

He stayed silent, and *that* didn't bode well to Mina.

"You like working that much?" she asked.

"I like staying busy…at least, I do lately."

Because of the scandal, but she wasn't going to mention it. Wasn't going to pop their bubble.

It seemed as if he'd just needed time to chew on her initial question—the one about vacation—and he swerved back around to answer it.

"Someday," he said, "I'd like to buy back the spread I gave up in Montana, then spend a lot of time there."

"Why didn't you keep it?"

"Because I didn't think I'd ever be going there again.

I really thought I could help my dad recover from cancer and we'd have this wonderful life down south." It was obvious that "dad" meant Abe, and it probably always would. "I can afford the land a hundred times over now, but..."

He didn't have to finish, didn't have to say that things were never going to go back to the way they'd been.

"What was your ranch like?"

"The Double R?" Chet tightened his arms around her. "Three hundred acres, a cabin that was built over a half century ago by a rancher who sold it to me after he retired. He was one of those old-time coots—you know, the kind you'd expect to see on a bench outside of a general store, whiling the hours away with a bunch of other oldsters who sit there spitting tobacco and exchanging gossip."

"Just like old pioneer women."

"Yeah. But these gossips would have scraggly beards down to their belts."

When he went quiet again, Mina could just about feel how much he missed his old home.

She leaned against his arms, enjoying the sensation of muscle, stalwartness. "You never would've left if it wasn't for Abe."

"Never. But I like Texas. And I'm okay at my job."

"You're more than okay. You're a natural at putting together development deals."

"Thanks."

She swallowed, getting to the bigger questions. "So you're going to stay for a while? In Texas?"

Although she didn't see him nod, she could sense it.

"I owe it to my brothers," he said. "And to Eli, even

if he's the one who made all this trouble. He's falling apart and I think the only thing that's going to bring him around is acceptance from all of us Barron boys."

She was so proud to hear him say that—to take matters in hand and turn them around. Shock had forced him away just after the scandalous truth had come out, anger had kept him on the periphery of his new family, doing what he could to help them but never fully allowing Eli the forgiveness he needed. But he sounded as if he was ready to tackle everything now.

That was another good sign for their future, yet time would tell if this was only pillow talk.

He was stroking her skin now, light fingertip brushes over her arms. Her pulse skittered, her flesh tightening with heat.

Until morning, she thought. That's what he'd promised her, and she was going to make him own up to it.

She stretched beneath him, angling her face so that her lips would meet his.

"I'm glad you're staying," she said against his mouth.

It turned into a kiss before she could say any more.

It wasn't easy to get out of bed come morning, but Chet forced himself to do it, even after awakening to the sight of Mina next to him.

The sheets gathered at her waist and her arms were flung over her head. Her positioning made her breasts all the more tempting, and he woke her up by kissing their pink tips.

She groaned, but when they both saw the time on his digital clock—6:07 a.m.—they got going soon enough.

Since he was leaving for the airport later today, neither of them made promises to meet again, just as they had last night. Nevertheless, being with her was all Chet could think about as Mina pulled her clothes on then rushed out of his cabin with a quick kiss to his cheek.

"See you at lunch?" she asked.

He knew that she had a meeting with some contractors in about forty-five minutes, and he would be dining with representatives from the nearby Chamber of Commerce at noon. Mina was scheduled to be there, too.

"See you then," he said, smiling, and that's the closest they got to making future plans.

After showering and putting on a gray business suit, Chet left the cabin. He even found his hat on the side of the path they'd traveled last night, and he beat it against the trunk of a tree instead of his leg, just to get the dew off. It might've even been the same tree he'd pressed Mina against when he'd kissed her.

He looked at it, hormones swirling around in him like fireflies.

Last night. God knew how he was going to get it out of his mind.

And he couldn't, though he put up a valiant effort while walking to his office, checking in with the main Barron headquarters via phone and then seeing to all the other projects he had going.

When lunchtime came around, he went to the dining room, which was one of the first areas to be fully decorated, with its elegant dark-paneled walls, Southwest-inspired art, massive fireplace and roses on every linen-covered table.

He arrived before any of the businessmen did, beating even Mina by a few minutes.

She was dressed in full business attire, too, in a dark blue suit with a lowered waist and wingtip pumps. The red hair that he'd combed his fingers through last night was pulled back in a pearl clip.

He wished he could just walk up to her and say, "Can't you wear it down?" As the businessmen arrived just after Mina, needles of emerging panic started to poke at Chet.

It was only during the meal itself that he got ahold of himself.

Work tended to do that though, whether it was out on the Montana range under the big blue sky or in an office. Still, he was all too aware of Mina as she sat at the other end of the table entertaining two men who owned local movie theaters.

He tried not to think about how taken they looked by Mina, how much attention they were paying to her beaming smile and bubbly laugh.

Good God, she was still in an afterglow and they couldn't help but respond to it.

Again, he thought about his mother—how she'd fooled Abe with her betrayal—and Chet fought to maintain the trust that Mina had built up in him again.

Mina wasn't like his mom. So why couldn't he remember that?

Somehow, Chet got through lunch and the niceties of escorting their guests to the resort limos that would drive them off and away. All the while, though, he kept an eye on Mina and those men.

They were the last to leave. One of them was even ruddy with all the whiskey he'd drunk.

He was wearing a hat with a snakeskin band and a

black suit. *An urban cowboy,* Chet thought, as the man whispered something in Mina's ear.

Chet had noticed that she'd refrained from alcohol during lunch, but that was Mina—always in control of business.

Except maybe for last night…

When she distanced herself from the man while still managing to seem friendly, the guy's associate, Todd Buckley, pulled him away.

"Come on, Jason. Time to leave our kind hosts."

Jason put an arm around Mina and she widened her eyes at Chet, who was just about to blow a gasket.

But this was business. A responsible tycoon wouldn't slam his fist into the face of one of the people he was trying to woo, now would he?

So he balanced his temper, went to the limo and pointedly opened the door.

"Great to see you, Jason," Chet said through gritted teeth. He nodded at the guy's friend. "Todd."

Todd Buckley pulled Jason inside as his buddy blew a kiss to Mina.

"Charmed," he said. "Everything about this place is charmed—"

Cutting him off, Chet shut the door and pounded on the top of the vehicle, letting the driver know it was safe to go.

When the limo was out of sight, Chet muttered, "Charmed. One more second of that nonsense and he would've been seeing stars, all right."

He'd said it low enough so that Mina probably hadn't heard. Even so, when she stood next to him, she had an air about her that he hadn't felt before—a sense that he'd claimed her, even outside of the bedroom, and she was claiming him right back.

That panic assaulted him once more.

With a slap of truth, he knew that *everyone,* whether they were a father or mother, had the capacity to betray. He'd already learned that well. So what the hell was he doing setting himself up for another fall, even if it was with a woman who seemed as if she wasn't capable of lying to him?

As some of the staff, including Danny Hogan, walked toward the restaurant, Chet tried not to act like a man in crisis.

Even though the whole thing about protecting Mina from office gossip—her sleeping her way to the top—struck false with Chet now, he realized that he truly didn't want the staff to know what had happened between them.

"Well," Mina said to him under her breath, "lunch sure was fun."

He tried to keep his dander down. "You handled Jason the drunk well."

"So did you."

She smiled up at him, showing him how she'd noticed that he'd barely contained himself with good old Jason, just as Danny shouted out a hello.

They waved, and Mina took a step away from Chet, as if she also was wary of causing office gossip.

For some reason, that was a warped relief. She wasn't going to announce their liaison. She wasn't going to press him, either, he hoped.

She'd been carrying that iPad at her side, just as she always did, and now she turned it on, accessing one of those images on the screen. He couldn't help but notice that it was as if she'd sensed all his panic and she was pretending it didn't matter.

"I need to get my schedule straight," she said, back to business. "Jeremiah's wedding is in a week…."

Wedding.

Last night, he'd invited her.

God, how deep was he going to get himself before things blew apart, as they definitely would? It was inevitable.

But he couldn't rescind his offer. Besides, she'd gotten an invitation herself, and she would be there, anyway.

"The wedding weekend starts next Saturday," he said. "I can arrange our transportation to Florence Ranch. You'll be back at the San Antonio offices by then, right?"

"Yes."

She seemed to notice this cooling off. Hesitating a moment, she started plugging away at that computer again.

Then she stopped, although she still stared at it.

Chet had a bad feeling about this.

"The thing is…" she said, halting as she bit her lower lip.

"What?" he asked.

She looked up at him, resolute in some way that he couldn't explain.

"I promised my parents I'd stop by their place on Friday night since it's on the way to your family's ranch," she said. "My dad's got his birthday coming up, but he and my mom will be away on a cruise on his big day. I thought I'd give him his present and eat some cake, just to celebrate with him."

What the hell else could Chet do—say no to her?

Half of him felt numb, the other half warmed up. He hadn't been to a girl's house and met her parents since…

Damn. High school. That was the last time he'd cottoned up to someone so thoroughly that he'd been summoned to meet the family.

"Feel free to make a change in plans," Mina said. She'd obviously noted Chet's minor freak-out, even though he'd done his best to hide it.

He gauged her expression. Casual.

Was he making too much out of this?

"Okay," he said. "Why not?"

He'd said it casually as well, and as they began walking to the administration offices, he thought he saw a flash of an unidentifiable emotion fly over her gaze.

But it was gone before he could be certain.

Chapter Six

Nearly a week later, the limo that had picked Mina and Chet up from the Barron offices drove down a white-fenced country lane, finally stopping in front of the Ferguson family home.

It wasn't anything fancy—just a beige, one-level ranch house set back on a couple of green acres and lined by oak trees. But as Chet stared out the window while they pulled into the long driveway, Mina wondered if he was getting the sense of stability she'd always felt when coming back here.

"So this is where you grew up," he said.

Mina nodded. "Not too far from the city, but just far enough in the country. We even had space for a horse. Lolly passed on years ago, just after me and my sisters moved out, and my parents never did buy another."

"Maybe you'll get a home someday that has enough room for your own horse."

"No one can replace Lolly."

She smiled at Chet, so glad to see him again. It'd seemed like months instead of just about a week since they'd parted ways for business purposes.

Sure, they hadn't had any big, romantic "nice to see you again" moment today when he'd brought her down from the office and to the waiting limo, but she was certain that was because there'd been Barron employees all around them. And during the drive, he'd been friendly enough.

Still, she kept thinking there was a little… Well, *distance* wasn't really the word. *Cool* wasn't a good way to describe it, either. But he sure wasn't acting like he wanted to whisk her off to bed again.

Maybe he would come to her after they got tucked into Florence Ranch tonight…

But they had to get through this visit to her childhood home first. It was an important night, although he didn't know it. She'd asked him here because she wanted to see how he got along with the family, if he could fit in someday.

The limo came to a stop, and Mina flattened her skirt, still grateful that her tummy hadn't "popped" yet. If she had, her mom, with her eagle eyes, probably would've noticed something going on with Mina, even if she'd worn baggier clothes.

Just hold on, she thought to her little passenger. *Help me out a little longer.*

As the driver opened the door for them, Mina poked out her head, seeing that her niece, Lizzie, was already sprinting out the perennial flower-decorated front entrance, dressed in her fairy dress with the wings flapping behind her.

But...*Lizzie?*

What was her niece doing here when Mina hadn't said anything to her mom about inviting Katie to this short-but-sweet hello for her dad's birthday?

"Mina!" the little girl shouted, crashing into Mina as she got out of the limo and hugging her legs so tightly that it was impossible to walk.

Mina bent down and embraced Lizzie, kissing her red-haired head. "Hey, there, Tinkerbell! Are you going to recreate your show from last week for me?"

"Yes!"

Lizzie backed up to get a good look at Mina, and the expression on her freckled face was so open and full of innocent love that it was almost heartbreaking. But in a way that let Mina know that she'd done something right to earn her niece's affection.

She fought the urge to rest her hands over her tummy, just to feel the other member of the family who would be joining them.

Lizzie was already staring at the limo, and at Chet, who'd come to stand beside Mina while he held the chocolate sheet cake and the wrapped present Mina had brought for her father—a computerized ebook reader that he could use on the cruise after she showed him how to work it tonight.

At Lizzie's unwavering curiosity with Chet, Mina fortified herself.

And so it would begin.

"Lizzie, this is Mr. Chet," Mina said. "I work with him."

Lizzie just smiled a little shyly and said a tiny, "Hi." For a rambunctious toddler, she could sure get quiet fast in front of strangers.

"We're on our way to a wedding," Mina added, as if she felt the need to explain it to a youngster. Then again, maybe she was just practicing for all the queries that were going to come from her family, since it looked like Katie was here.

Darn her mom. She'd sounded the alarms for the troops to check out the man Mina had finally brought home. There would be *lots* of explaining to do tonight.

"What's a wedding?" Lizzie asked.

"It's where there's a bride dressed in a beautiful white dress," Mina said. "You went to Aunt Amy's wedding a few months ago, and you've seen pictures from your mommy and daddy's."

"Oh, yeah."

Chet had gotten to a knee to bring himself to Lizzie's height, and Mina's chest closed in on itself.

"Hi there, Lizzie," he said, extending his hand for a shake.

The little girl returned his greeting, but just as quickly rushed back to Mina, burying her face in her aunt's long skirt.

Mina grinned at Chet, who was rising to his feet.

"Don't worry," she said. "Lizzie's going to be your best friend in about ten minutes."

"I'll be ready for it."

He'd better be, along with fortifying himself against the rest of the brood.

"Lizzie," she said, "did I tell you that Chet has a new niece? A baby?"

The little girl peeked at him, her interest awakened.

Chet said, "Her name's Caroline."

Lizzie let go of Mina's skirt a bit. "She's a *baby?*"

He laughed. "She's my brother Jeremiah's pride and joy."

By then, Mina's parents had come out the front door. Her mother, whose red hair was just beginning to be paled by strands of gray, made a beeline for Mina. Meanwhile, her dad made his way down the brick front steps, limping slightly, his salt-and-pepper hair in a buzz cut. Sometimes his joints got stiff, and it looked like today was one of those days.

After her mom enfolded her in a hug, Mina went to her father, greeting him the same way.

"Happy early birthday, Dad," she said into his shoulder.

When the hug ended, he said, "Good that you got to stop by before your mom drags me off on that boat for parts unknown."

Mom rolled her eyes. "Yes, I'm torturing him with this vacation. It's such a hardship."

He shrugged good-naturedly, and both her parents rested their attention on Chet...and that limousine.

Now the fun would *really* start.

"This is my boss," Mina said. She'd only told her mom that they were able to stop by tonight because the house was on the way to Florence Ranch. However, she hadn't said anything about Chet being more than a carpool buddy for the wedding. She'd even told her mom not to read anything into the visit.

Didn't matter though, because her mother had obviously conjured her own interpretation of tonight, since this was the cowboy Katie had spied during her computer call with Mina. From the "Hallelujah, my daughter's actually brought a man home!" look on her face, Mina knew that Mom was in heaven.

She and Dad welcomed Chet with open arms, and he took it in stride.

Had she set him up unfairly though, testing him to see how much he could take before she unleashed even bigger things on him? Was he thinking that, after their second night together, she had turned into some nut job who'd assumed that they were engaged now and was whisking him into a situation that he wasn't ready for?

As everyone headed for the house, Mina kept Chet behind for a second.

"They don't know anything intimate about my personal life," she whispered.

What she meant was that they didn't know *much* about him and her.

He paused, and she just had enough to time hold her breath before he said, "It's okay. It's good to meet them." As she exhaled, he added, "Now I see where you get that hair."

A joke. He was using his sense of humor to ease the moment. But that was another good sign, wasn't it? He wasn't running back to the limo or anything.

Slow and easy, she thought. *Just keep it going that way.*

She crossed her fingers in front of her as Chet ushered her inside the door, to a hall with antique pitchers on old pine nightstands, plus a hat and coatrack where Chet deposited his Stetson. As they moved through the prairie-influenced living room, with its cow skull wall and wagon wheel wall hangings, the aroma of barbecue floated in the air.

When Mina heard more voices around the corner,

in the direction of the kitchen, she shot her mom the stink eye from behind. Her mother had invited Katie *and* Amy.

Mina took up Chet's side as her sisters peered around the corner, then came at her with arms extended.

"There she is!" Katie said, her unbound strawberry-blond hair brushing Mina's cheek as they hugged.

Amy, who'd just graduated from college earlier in the year and had gotten married right after, took Katie's place. She'd cut her black hair short, in a bob, since the last time Mina had seen her.

"What's this?" Mina asked, ruffling her younger sister's locks.

Amy shrugged away from Mina. "Scott likes it."

"Where is Scott?" Mina glanced at Katie. "And Jonathan?"

"The hubbies stayed at home," Katie said with a twinkle in her eyes that told Mina that the "hubbies" weren't quite as interested as their wives were in checking out Mina's traveling companion.

You'd think Mina was an old maid with all the fuss being put out over Chet. Then again, it'd been about a year since Mina had even talked about a man to her family. And before Michael, she'd been just as inactive.

They were only excited for her.

More introductions were made, and it didn't escape Mina's attention that Katie and Amy were in full inspection mode, looking Chet up and down, then trading a subtle, meaningful glance while Chet was otherwise occupied.

She wanted to ask them to tone it down, but that would require some privacy, and she wasn't about to let Chet out of her line of sight right now.

Lizzie was holding up her hands for Mina to lift her, so she scooped up her niece, saying, "Oh, my, you're getting to be such a big girl. When did you grow up so fast?"

"I don't know," Lizzie said.

Her mom had already relieved Chet of the cake and birthday gift and gone for some martini glasses in the freezer. Taking the cue, Katie was using the shaker to do some mixing.

"Let's go to the patio for cocktails," Mom said. "We'll eat out there, too, and catch the last of this good weather."

"Dinner?" Mina asked. "Mom, we can't stay *that* long."

"Sure you can." Mom glanced at Chet.

He slid a look to Mina, the familiar sparkle that she hadn't seen so much of lately in his eyes. Just witnessing it again turned her heart up at the corners.

"Dinner would be great," he said. "I'll just phone my brothers and let them know."

Mom looked mightily satisfied at that.

Katie put down the shaker. "Who wants a 'tini?"

Everyone but Mina accepted the offer, and when her mom gave her an inquisitive glance, Mina gestured to Lizzie.

"We pixies are going to have Woodland Punch instead."

Her niece clapped her hands as Katie said, "Suit yourself," and poured.

Soon enough, Mom, Katie, Amy and Dad went outside to the patio, where he said he needed to check the grill. That left Mina and Chet behind with Lizzie, and as he watched Mina with her niece, she thought she saw a certain appreciation in his gaze.

"What?" Mina asked.

The moment passed, and he shook his head. "It's nothing."

But she couldn't ignore the look she'd seen.

Was she just imagining it?

A short time later, out on the patio, Chet stood near the barbecue with Mina's dad, Ewan, as he minded the carne asada. Nearby, the bulk of the Ferguson women sipped their martinis while Mina and Lizzie partook of their Woodland Punch, which was nothing more than fruit juice with a maraschino cherry.

Ewan grinned at Chet, holding up his barbecue tongs. "Bet the last thing you were expecting to eat in the Ferguson household was Mexican food."

"I hadn't thought about it, really."

"Well, we've got some haggis in the fridge if you're in the mood."

Before Chet even answered, Ewan said, "Just a joke. In spite of our Scots blood, we're not much for sheep guts and Highland grub around here."

"What did you say, Ewan?" Mina's mom, Lorna, called out.

"Nothing, dear." He winked at Chet.

No wonder Mina had grown up so well. Judging from her family, they were a spirited, loving bunch, and when Mina commented about how they were perhaps a little too invested in her private life, Chet understood why.

Some families were like that. They looked out for each other, even after the kids left the roost. Abe and Laura had done that for Chet up in Montana to some extent. Hell, Abe had even procured Chet the job of a lifetime before he died, making sure that he would be set up in this new family of his—the one with Eli as a father.

Sure, Abe's gesture was touching, but it still angered Chet to have been left in the dark for so long when it came to knowing his true parentage. And he was enraged for Abe's sake, too. He hurt for him, because no man should've had to endure the humiliation he'd gone through with a cheating wife and brother.

Ewan broke into Chet's musing. "You're off to a wedding then?"

"Yeah. Florence Ranch is about a half hour away."

"Near Duarte Hill. I've been to that town. Quaint, isn't it? Still looks like there could be gunfights in the streets there."

Katie's voice interrupted. "Is that where you grew up, Chet? Duarte Hill?"

"No. My parents raised me on a ranch on the other side of San Antonio. My…other family lives near Duarte Hill."

Chet had the feeling there'd be questions during this visit. Actually, he'd guessed that this dinner wasn't really so much a "meet the boss" moment so much as Mina bringing him to her family—her support system—so they could get a general view of him.

Yup, now that he really thought about it, he'd had that suspicion the moment she'd asked him, but he'd still come. Why? He just wasn't sure.

Or maybe he *wanted* to meet the family.…

He took a drink. Damn it, he didn't know where his head was. But the one thing he was sure of was that it would be a long time before he would be able to really commit to anyone.

Maybe he was making too much out of this visit, anyway. It could be that Mina truly *had* merely wanted to say "Happy Birthday" to her dad before her parents left on their cruise this weekend, and these traveling plans had matched perfectly with her needs.

Yeah, he thought, getting less antsy the more he thought about it. This was nothing to get worried about.

Little Lizzie had finished her punch by now and she was trying to pull Mina out of her chair.

"Come play with me."

"But..." Mina pointed to her unfinished glass of Woodland Punch, yet Chet could tell she wouldn't ever say no to her niece.

"Pleeeease?"

When Mina stood, Lizzie jumped up and down, her red ponytail bobbing. Then she went around to her grandma and tugged her up, too.

Like most grandmas, this one was only too happy to oblige.

When Lizzie got to her mom and Aunt Amy, both women held up their martinis.

"Maybe another time," Amy said.

Katie stretched out her legs in front of her. "We'll watch from here."

Undeterred, Lizzie brought her grandma and Mina out to the grass, where she proceeded to perform some kind of cute fairy dance. Mina stood there, hands clasped over her chest, so obviously adoring of her niece that Chet found himself looking at her as he'd done earlier when she'd been holding Lizzie in her arms.

Someday, some guy and some family would be real lucky to have her. She was meant to have children, meant to love them.

Chet just wished he was the man who could give her all that, but it was just a fantasy for now. There was a chance it might always be, too, because after the initial bloom of happiness, he might only end up dragging her into his sorry affairs, and what family needed *that?*

But there was something else, too—something that kept eating at him until he couldn't ignore it.

Deep inside, he kept thinking about what his mom had done to his dad.

Amy spoke. "So you've been working with Mina for a while now, Chet?"

"Months."

At the grill, Ewan glanced at Amy over his shoulder, then went back to the meat, taking it off and transferring it to a plate. "How's our superstar doing for you?"

Superstar. It sounded as if they held Mina on a pedestal, but she'd told Chet about how she'd always strived to be her best for them. Maybe that was what her family expected of her, too.

Chet smiled. "I couldn't ask for a better coworker. I'm lucky she was assigned to me."

"Damn lucky," Katie said as she traced the rim of her martini glass.

When she jerked in her seat, Chet wondered if it was because Amy had kicked her older sister under the table.

Katie sent a sweet grin to him, then said, "We're just huge Mina fans."

"That's right," Amy said. "And she's the same with us.

We're all close. Just like this." She wound her forefinger and middle finger together.

A tweak of longing got to Chet. His family—back when he'd thought it *was* his family—had been knit looser than the Fergusons, like a sweater that you could still wear, even though it'd started falling apart.

Katie chimed in again. "You'd mentioned something about your 'other' family, Chet? The ones that live near Duarte Hill?"

He should've just shut his big mouth earlier. They'd probably heard about the scandal and were starting to dig for more information, looking out for their sister.

"Extended family," he said vaguely.

Ewan broke in at that point, bringing the meat to the table and covering it with some tinfoil. "Next I'll hear you asking him how much he makes per year and what color toothpaste he likes to use."

"Dad..." both girls said.

He turned to Chet. "I could use some help plating the side dishes and bringing them out."

Thank goodness. "Consider me employed."

Chet nodded to Katie and Amy, then followed Ewan into the house.

Mina watched as Chet went inside with her dad, leaving Katie and Amy to chat in low tones with each other.

"They grilled him," she said in a near whisper to her mom as Lizzie performed her open house dance for them about ten feet away. "I knew I shouldn't have left him alone."

"He's a big boy, Mina."

"Why'd you have to invite them over?"

"They heard you were coming and there was no stopping them. You know your sisters."

"Yes—they're married. And once a woman gets married, she starts to wage a campaign for everyone else to get hitched, too."

She sounded testy. Maybe all her frustration with Chet was coming out now.

Lizzie paused in her dancing, and Mina and her mom clapped, encouraging the little girl to continue.

A second later, Mom said, "Sweetheart, you wouldn't have brought him home if there wasn't a reason."

Mina wanted to tell all, but then again, she didn't. Telling would put all her hopes and dreams for Chet out there in the open. It would expose a truth that she hadn't even addressed with Chet yet.

Worse yet, she was concerned about what her mom—her family—might think about her being with this scandal-ridden man.

She decided to meet her mom halfway.

"Okay, maybe he's a little more than a boss to me."

"And…?" her mom goaded.

That was enough information for now. "Mom, I don't know where this is going to lead."

She didn't add that this wasn't *exactly* the truth. It would lead to a baby soon enough.

Lizzie spotted a squirrel down the lawn and ditched the dancing to get nearer to it.

"Lizzie," Grandma said, "don't get too close."

The girl came to a skidding halt but still watched the squirrel with fascination.

Then Mina's mom smoothly transitioned back to the former conversation. "The course of true love never did run smooth, Mina."

"Tell me about it. It's just that Chet has got a…complicated life. More than most."

"I'm aware of the Barron scandal. And I'm sure Amy and Katie were back there trying to get to the bottom of it."

All right. This talk wasn't going so badly. If her family had heard about the scandal and they hadn't given him the third degree before even letting him in the house, that was a positive sign.

Her mom saw how she was watching her sisters again. "Your dad was there, too, and he clearly took Chet out of the line of fire."

"You mean the lion's den."

Her mom put an arm around her. "They mean well."

"At least *you're* not giving him grief."

"Why should I? I saw right away how he looks at you."

A flash of tiny fireworks lit her up inside. "What do you mean?"

"Please, Mina. He can't take his eyes off of you."

The fireworks continued in her, turning into the kind that zoomed and circled their way into the sky.

Her mom patted her on the shoulder, then removed her arm from around her. "He might be going through some significant troubles, but you can't tell it. He carries himself well. I like that. He gives me a good mom-feeling."

"He carries himself that way in public. But when he's out of it…" She thought of the night he'd come to her, a broken man.

"He lets you see him when his shields come down?"

"Yes."

"Then it sounds as if you don't have too much work to do with him besides waiting for his mind to catch up with his heart. And, unlike Michael, I can tell Chet's heart is with you."

It was about the last thing she expected her mom to say.

Wasn't her mom going to warn her, point out all of Chet's shortcomings in order to save her the sorrow?

Mina stuffed her hands in her skirt pockets. "I expected this to be harder, introducing him to you."

"Why?"

She sent her mom a caustic glance.

Her mother seemed taken aback. "Are you *that* worried about our stamp of approval?"

"You haven't ever been shy about giving it."

"Mina." Her mom sounded surprised. "You've always been so independent, as if you didn't mind so much what we think."

That's because she'd trained herself to feel that way for a long time, ever since she'd overheard her inebriated uncle at that barbecue.

It'd have been a shame if that little girl hadn't been born, he'd said to a cousin who hadn't known anything about the family secret as they'd lingered over beers. He'd gone on to explain how Lorna and Ewan had gotten the news one day and they'd decided to keep Mina, as if she'd been some kind of package delivered to their door by mistake and they'd warmed up to the contents enough not to send it back.

How could Mina ever tell her mom how that had felt? Nobody even knew that Mina had overheard while climbing under the nearby tables, playing hide-and-seek with the other kids. And she'd carried the secret with her for years, trying to please her parents, half afraid that they would, somehow, send her back.

She'd gone on to please everyone else, too.

A mix of anger and sadness crept up her throat as she thought of her child. He or she would grow up knowing they were wanted through and through, no matter what happened with Chet. It'd taken this accidental pregnancy, her own baby, to dredge up all her old feelings, but maybe that was a good thing.

Maybe it would force her to solve some of her own issues before her child was even born.

Needing some alone time, Mina began to walk back to the patio. "I've always cared what you thought, Mom."

"Mina."

Her soft voice stopped Mina, and she glanced back to find her mother's eyes teary.

"Don't listen to what *we* have to say," she said. "Because no matter what you decide, we'll be there to support you, not to give you more grief. Surely you know that."

Mina wondered if that would be the case even if they knew that their superstar daughter had been silly enough to have gotten pregnant when the father might not even love her.

Chapter Seven

Dinner at the Fergusons' went by without another hitch for Chet, mainly because Ewan kept training a fatherly "watch what you say" gaze on Katie and Amy for the next couple of hours.

Instead, Chet enjoyed talking about the cruise that Mr. and Mrs. Ferguson were going on—a long jaunt to the Caribbean. He liked how there was a teasing sense of adoration between everyone in the family, and he got the feeling that they would go to war for each other if it came right down to it.

And that was what really struck him. They'd go to war *for* each other, not against each other.

After the meal—and after a crash course that Mina held for her father for his new e-book reader—Chet and Mina were on the road to Duarte Hill and Florence Ranch again, where Chet just wasn't sure there would be the same loving atmosphere.

Outside the limo windows, darkness made the white fences into ghostly tracks along the road. Mina sat across from him, watching the scenery go by, a thoughtful expression on her face—one that just about wrenched Chet's heart because it turned the tips of her mouth down instead of up.

"Your family's good people," he said. "I'm glad you brought me along tonight."

Leaning her head back on the seat, she turned her gaze to him. "I'm glad you came."

She didn't say anything else about it, but Chet got the feeling that there was a lot more going through her mind than her dad's birthday and the cruise her parents would be taking.

"You all right?" he asked.

"Sure." She paused as the limo hummed underneath them, tires over blacktop. Then she said, "It's just…I had a little talk with my mom, and it made me realize something that I didn't expect."

"What's that?"

She tucked an auburn strand of hair behind her ear, as if it was a good excuse to hesitate again. "She said that their opinions shouldn't matter so much to me. At first, I interpreted that to mean that I wasn't important enough to care about. It stunned me. But when I started to really think about it, I understood that she *didn't* mean it that way."

"And?"

Mina looked so forlorn on the other side of the limo. "It really drove home how I've always believed that I was something my parents had to get used to, something they had to fit into their lives, like a square peg in a round hole, so I tend to overreact about how *they* react to things. I suppose I've even come to like how the family is so protective and interested in everything I do, because it shows that they actually want me."

Chet leaned forward. "Everyone in that family thinks the world of you, Mina. You have to talk yourself into recognizing that?"

"I guess. Especially since Katie and Amy never had any big realization like mine, as far as I know. My parents were financially ready for another child when it came time for Amy, years later."

"I doubt your parents ever even think of what happened with you."

"You're right." She looked out the window again. "It's amazing to realize that I've spent so much of my life trying so hard to please them so they'd never regret having me."

Her words were a slight hit to his gut. "A man and woman should never regret having a child."

It'd just come out, bald and truthful.

As she watched him, her gaze was forthright. "No, they shouldn't."

Was she thinking about him now, and not her own life? Thinking about how he might've felt the night when Abe and Eli had taken him into a private room and told him who he really was?

Mina seemed ready to say something else—something with major substance to it, because he could almost feel it in the air between them.

But then she went quiet again, and Chet respected her silence, leaning back, his mind stretched in a million different directions.

And every one of them seemed to lead to Florence Ranch.

* * *

The ranch was smack-dab in Texas Hill Country, reigning on the top of a rise, surrounded by pines, a creek, meadows and guest cottages. There was even a swimming hole nearby—a place Chet had visited a few times during his youth when Eli would invite Abe and his family over.

More innocent times, as far as Chet had known.

The limo climbed the driveway up to the Greek Revival mansion, known affectionately as the "big house," and Chet couldn't help but think about how different it was from the home of Mina's parents, which had been far more modest and…

Well, cozy.

Theirs was a house that was more on par with his old cabin up in Montana. No fuss. No fancy stuff. Just a place to wander around in at your leisure, a place to set your boots in without having to worry about how they might dirty up the floor.

After the limo came to a halt, Chet didn't wait for the driver to open the door. He exited first, extending his hand to help Mina out of the vehicle.

When she alighted, she ran her gaze over the mansion, then removed her hand from his.

"I can never get used to this place," she said.

"Same here." And that was the truth. Every time he arrived, he felt like a visitor, even after all these months of knowing that he should belong.

The driver went to get their bags, and Chet took them from the guy, thanking him and letting him go to his cabin down the hill for the night. He was a Barron employee, so he stayed on the property, just as the ranch hands and other staff did.

While Chet and Mina climbed the few stairs that led to the entry, the front door opened.

It was Tyler, Chet's oldest half brother.

"Here they are." Tall and solidly built in his jeans and Western shirt, Tyler's coloring resembled Aunt Florence's, with their dark brown hair and green eyes. He didn't have much of Eli in him at all—not like Chet and Jeremiah did.

After Chet hung his hat and coat on an intricate iron rack, Tyler took his bag from him, then enveloped him in a fraternal hug. Chet was getting used to this kind of thing, so he returned the gesture, lingering for a second longer than he usually did.

Tyler seemed to notice, and he grinned, turning to Mina.

"We're really glad you could come this weekend."

"Are you kidding?" she said. "I wouldn't miss a Barron wedding."

He embraced her, too, then guided them to the lounge.

"Why don't y'all get settled in there," Tyler said. "Millie will have your bags taken to your quarters in the meantime."

Millie was the household manager. Chet knew that she would send his things to the room that was on constant standby for him here in the mansion. Mina had been assigned a guest cottage.

Without thinking, he put his hand on the small of Mina's back, intending to escort her into the lounge just behind Tyler.

Did she haul in a breath?

Removing his hand out of pure instinct—pure preservation, really—he followed her into the lounge, with its dark-wooded grandeur and velvet furnishings. Over a roaring fire, a painting of the "former" Barron family hung over the mantel: Eli, Aunt Florence, Tyler and Jeremiah.

Every time Chet saw it, he felt like a ghost in the portrait, felt just as empty inside of himself, too.

But he didn't have much time to think about that tonight, because everyone in the room—Jeremiah, his fiancée, Ally, and Zoe—came over to greet them.

Eli wasn't anywhere around, though.

Would he be able to get out of rehab to attend the wedding?

Jeremiah, who was taller than Chet by a couple of inches, though they resembled each other in so many other ways, slapped him on the back just before going to the minibar and getting out two glasses. Since he'd come straight from the office, he was dressed in a designer suit.

"My best man made it," he said to Chet.

Tyler cleared his throat. "*Co*-best man."

"That's what I meant." Jeremiah addressed Chet and Mina. "So what's your poison tonight?"

Chet waited for Mina to answer before he did.

"Nothing for me right now," she said.

He wasn't much in the mood for drinking, either. The weekend would be bringing a lot of opportunities for that.

"I'm good," he said.

Ally was holding a whiskey, just like Jeremiah. The fancy cut crystal glass went along well with her Grace Kelly looks—the long, straight platinum hair, a high-class bearing.

"Caroline's already asleep," she said, referring to the

newborn she'd adopted recently, before she and Jeremiah had fallen in love and decided to get married. "I wish she could've stayed up to see her future uncle."

Uncle. Chet liked the sound of that. Liked that whenever he got the chance to see Caroline, which wasn't often since Jeremiah and Ally sometimes lived in California, the baby smiled at him, making him a little lighter, too.

"I'll see her first thing tomorrow." Then Chet said to Mina, "You should get a load of Caroline. She's the cutest thing in creation."

"Except for Lizzie," Mina said, grinning.

"Of course." Chet laughed.

Zoe, Tyler's wife, said, "Sounds to me like you're a regular sucker for children, Chet." Her gray-blue eyes sparkled against her olive skin and shoulder-length dark hair. She was giving Chet and Mina "that" look, as if she'd already assumed he had brought a date to this wedding, that he and Mina might even be serious enough to have mentioned the possibility of having children one day.

What the hell?

Mina had shifted position, as if she felt the scrutiny. And why not, when they *all* obviously thought there was something going on? He could tell by the way they treated Mina—Zoe and Ally giving her those sisterly smiles, although this was the first time Mina had met Ally. Tyler and Jeremiah were even exchanging "uh-huh" glances with each other. And, this, after Chet had already told his brothers over the phone that he and Mina were traveling together because it was convenient.

Not that he thought that they were going to buy that or anything. But he tried.

Chet shuffled his booted feet. All right, so the "convenience" explanation had been a flat-out lie. He wouldn't have asked Mina in the heat of the moment that one night if he didn't feel right about it. It was just… Well, he didn't know what to do with her *now,* whether he dared to ever touch her again when he knew damned well that it would lead to some tough questions for him, like what if he couldn't get his act together?

When the women led Mina to a leather couch near the flickering fire, Chet couldn't help but to follow her with his gaze.

Unfortunately, Tyler and Jeremiah noticed.

Chet cut them off at the pass by clearing his throat. His brothers got the message, keeping their opinions to themselves.

There were more important things to talk about, anyway.

"Where's Eli?" he asked.

Jeremiah shot another look to Tyler, who nodded, as if he was telling his brother to go ahead.

"He's not here tonight," Jeremiah said, "but he's got a pass from the rehab center for the rest of the weekend."

Tyler added, "He'll be here tomorrow evening for the rehearsal dinner in town."

"Chet?" Jeremiah asked. "Is that okay?"

"Yes. I'm not going to make this difficult for everyone, especially during your wedding, Jeremiah." He looked up. "I'm finally going to make things right between me and Eli. It's well past time."

Tyler put a hand on Chet's shoulder, and Jeremiah patted his other arm. Brothers. Chet wasn't even going to think of them as half siblings anymore. Not if he wanted them all to come together.

He really was ready to face that.

Jeremiah held up his whiskey, as did Tyler. A toast, sealing a silent promise—one that Chet regretted having put off for this long.

Near the fireplace, Ally and Zoe were chatting up Mina pretty well. Mina looked comfortable with the others, smiling and talking just as if she belonged.

He watched the fire play with the color of her hair, watched how she tilted back her head every time she laughed. She fit in, all right, and for some reason, it sent a flood of warmth through him.

Being here on Florence Ranch was only highlighting how Tyler and Jeremiah had something with Zoe and Ally that Chet had never experienced. One look at Mina sitting so naturally among them made Chet think that everyone could have what his brothers did, even during the crisis they'd been surviving for the past months.

Everyone—even Chet.

Jeremiah, the scamp, was unable to hold back any longer. "Careful, Chet—the women are warming up to your assistant pretty thoroughly."

At the blunt observation, a familiar panic attacked once again. "Mina is just here because she's..."

Chet tripped over his words, and before he could search for the right ones, Jeremiah supplied them.

"Because she's your date?"

Straight-to-the-point Tyler looked baffled. "*Isn't* that what she is, Chet?"

Yes. No.

Damn it.

Chet turned his back on the women and lowered his

voice. "I'm not sure how to define it, so let's not define it at all, okay?"

His brothers just drank their cocktails, though Jeremiah smirked behind his glass.

There wasn't much else to say, not right now, when Chet didn't have anything figured out. All he knew was that he wanted to glance behind him again, keep Mina in his sights, because whenever she was in them, he felt better about life in general.

And about himself, too.

Mina and Chet hadn't stayed too long in the lounge. They'd bunked down in their respective rooms, and Mina had taken to her guest cottage like a bee to honey.

Her bed had soft sheets and was surrounded by pastel, sunrise artwork. She had a little kitchen where she could see bright flowers peeking out of a window box just outside, framing a view of the big house. It was "rustic chic," with a farmhouse-type minikitchen, complete with an old-fashioned lantern hanging over the stove.

She had just about everything she needed but Chet, who'd only said a quiet good-night to her before Millie, the household manager, had walked her to the cottage, explaining where things were and how to work them before leaving.

But why had Mina expected Chet to be in her cottage tonight when he'd come "home," to where all his problems were?

Even though her pulse limped along at his absence, she got a decent night's sleep, awakening just after dawn to a cloud-strung sky outside. After she got ready for the day, she went outside to sit on the stoop, drinking a mug of herbal tea that steamed in the cool morning.

It wasn't but fifteen minutes later that she witnessed Chet sauntering by on a nearby path, garbed in cowboy gear and carrying a fishing pole and tackle box in either hand.

Boom went her heart, and it didn't calm down, even as he walked farther and farther away.

Well, this wouldn't do—her on one side of the ranch and him on the other. She would never get him to see that he needed her in his life.

She set down her mug and walked as fast as she could to catch up to him, her skirt swishing around her legs and boots. The nippiness of the morning tweaked her arms, which were bared by her big, short-sleeved T-shirt, but she didn't go back for a sweater.

"Morning," she called out.

He stopped in his tracks, looking over his shoulder.

Was there a *boom* moment in him, too?

"I thought you'd be sleeping in," he finally said.

"A girl can only slumber for so many hours."

He stood there a second longer, then nodded to her.

"Okay, then," he said, and it sounded like a dismissal. "There're horses in the stables if you want a ride. Lots of room for walking until our car leaves for the rehearsal dinner at six sharp."

"I'm invited to the dinner?" She'd thought the wedding summons had been just that—for the ceremony and reception, not for the family events.

He looked bewildered. "Of course."

She held back a smile. Chet wasn't making a big deal out of it, but this made her his date. It really did.

He cleared his throat, then tipped his hat to her with the hand that carried the tackle box. "I'll see you then."

"I heard there's a cute fishing hole on the property." She didn't want him to go. "Is that where you're off to?"

"A *cute* fishing hole?" he asked.

This certainly didn't feel like a date, with him clearly just dying to get going.

But Mina was tired of this limbo. She'd come here to get to the bottom of him, and he wasn't going to slip away that easily.

She was gradually finding out that the more personal room she gave Chet Barron, the more skittish he got. Obviously, a woman couldn't grant him too much time to think.

"I'd like to see where you're off to, if you don't mind," she said, walking over to him. "I grew up in the suburbs, remember? Fishing holes are a curiosity to me."

"All I do is use the pole to put the hook in the water, Mina. It's not a big event or anything."

"I know, I know—and too much talk scares the fish away, so I'll keep chatter to a minimum."

He spread out an arm, inviting her to walk next to him.

There was a slight bounce in her step as they strolled down a path that cut through the grass as it turned from a manicured lawn to that of a meadow.

"Last night," she said, getting the "chatter" out of the way before they got to the fishing hole, "Ally asked if I'd like to hang around while she gets ready tomorrow. I thought that was nice of her."

Chet kind of grunted, and she didn't know what to make of that.

"I guess," she added, "that she just wants me to feel

included for some reason." She realized she was twisting the hem of her T-shirt and stopped.

"She asked you to join her because she likes you." He slowed their pace, came to a halt. "And because we arrived together."

"In the same car." Testing. Test, test.

"No, *together* together."

So he was admitting it—that this *was* a date.

She wanted to bust out and ask, *So what exactly does this mean?*

But her common sense said that she had him on a hook, and it was quite possible that he would find a way off of it if she pushed him. The truth was that Chet had actually come a decent way recently, and she just had to get him a little further in.

Just a little.

But, much to her surprise, he was the one who went forward.

"I haven't been honest with myself lately, but I'm trying, Mina. Bit by bit, with my real father, my situation in life...my relationship with you...I'm trying."

She nodded, letting him go on.

"I want to be with you," he said, his gaze wounded, confused. "But I'm not sure if I'm in any shape for it. That's why I've been hanging back."

"You haven't hung back all of the time." She meant about how they'd been intimate, how he'd given her his body, but not anything else, at the resort.

"You're right," he said. "I haven't."

He sounded like he was being hard on himself, just as he'd been when he'd apologized right after the first time they'd made love.

The last thing she wanted was to regress back to those

days, so she reached out, touched his arm, showing him how she appreciated his efforts.

"You *are* trying," she repeated. "That's all I can ask right now."

He didn't say anything, and she tightened her grip on him.

"You're going to make it through everything, Chet. I'll be damned if you don't."

As if he'd come to the end of what he had to say for now, he faintly smiled, then walked on.

Progress, she thought. They were getting there.

They took a path that led downhill, toward a bunch of cottonwoods. Soon they came to a secluded pond with large rocks jutting into the water. A particular flat one made for a perfect seat, so they headed toward it.

To get there, they had to negotiate some smaller rocks that peered just above the water.

"Careful," he said.

She waited until he went first, and he offered his hand to her for balance.

But when she went to take it, her foot slipped.

As she went down, all she could think was, *My baby...*

Chet grabbed for her, barely getting hold of her arm. She slid partway into the water anyway, dousing her bottom half.

She sat there in the shallow water, realizing that she wasn't hurt. Just...embarrassed.

"Are you all right?" he asked, helping her out of the water and to a stand.

Everything was steeped: her boots, her skirt, the bottom part of her T-shirt. Dripping wet.

She was only starting to comprehend how thoroughly

her clothing was leeched to her when Chet ran a gaze down her body.

Too late, she laid an arm over her tummy.

Her T-shirt-plastered tummy, which wasn't showing a pregnancy as much as…

Well, as much as it just *felt* pregnant with him standing here looking at her.

This was like the day in the Paradise Room, when she'd instinctively thought to hide her secret from him, no matter how her belly looked.

She started back to shore, treading through the shallow water, praying that he hadn't noticed anything strange about her reaction, hoping against hope.

"Great," she said, trying to divert his attention. "I really liked these boots, too."

"You sure you're okay?"

"Definitely," she answered, "but I'm not hanging around here looking like a drowned rat."

If he noticed her babbling, he didn't remark on it, and she left as quickly as she could, wondering just how much longer her secret was going to hold up.

Chapter Eight

During the rehearsal dinner at a lively Mexican restaurant in nearby Duarte Hill, Chet leaned against a planked wall, watching Mina talking with Ally and Zoe across the room.

Right now, she was wearing one of those full skirts she liked—this one white, with a pink shawl dipping down over her shoulders and to her hips.

But this morning…

This morning she'd been a little more exposed, when she'd slipped into the water and her T-shirt had stuck to her skin.

The way she'd acted, hugging an arm over her lower stomach… It'd been a repeat of her reaction that day he'd come upon her at the resort, in the Paradise Room, when she'd been wearing a bathing suit. He hadn't noted anything out of the ordinary that day, but now that she'd repeated the gesture so obviously, his mind started spinning a reason for it. It was almost as if she was deliberately covering something up.

As if she were…

Pregnant?

He'd seen pregnant women touch their stomachs just as Mina had, back in Montana, wives of friends, but in Mina's case the notion was absolutely ridiculous, and as soon as he'd even thought it, he'd pushed it away. Hell, if she was with child, it would've happened months ago, when they'd first been together, and he'd worn a condom, for heaven's sake.

But that wasn't the biggest reason he'd dismissed the temporary suspicion so quickly. Condoms could fail, but he'd come to believe that Mina, out of anyone in this world, would never *ever* pull the wool over his eyes, keeping that big of a secret from him. She wasn't like his mother, who'd once lied to his dad about the affair with Eli. She'd done the same to Chet, as well, until Abe had come clean with the truth.

No, if *anyone* could be trusted with anything, it was Mina, he told himself for what seemed like the millionth time.

Nonetheless, Chet's insides were scrambled. See what his problems did? They tainted more than just him. They carried over to the people who didn't deserve to be judged or under suspicion.

He looked across the room again, past the red, yellow, blue and green lanterns hanging from the ceiling, casting rainbow shadows over the distressed hardwood floor and rustic tables.

Mina.

He thought about what he would've done if she had gotten pregnant that night, or the second one, and…

The image of a little redheaded baby floated over his mind's eye, and Chet smiled.

It disappeared quickly enough, though. It was a good thing that she wasn't pregnant. As if they needed more complications…

While she solidified in his sight again, part of Chet wanted to apologize to her for all he'd put her through and for thinking even for a second that she would lie. The other part told him that there was no harm done, that he should just continue to stand in his corner and listen to the mariachi band as they sauntered around the room with their guitars, trumpets and violins, serenading the crowd now that the dinner had ended.

A voice brought him out of his musings. Jeremiah, who slung an arm around Chet.

"How's my co-best man?" he asked.

Chet put on a smile. "He's hoping he'll remember his cues tomorrow at the ceremony."

"You did just fine during the rehearsal." Jeremiah clinked nonalcoholic beer bottles with his brother. "This is my last night as a free man, so I want you to live it up right along with me. Ready to go yet?"

Chet sent him a look that said, *You're happy to get married, so cut the bull.*

Jeremiah laughed at the obvious truth, dropping his arm from around Chet's shoulders. "Just be ready to leave in about fifteen minutes."

"You got it."

Since all Jeremiah and Ally's most loved friends and relatives were in the area for the wedding, they were both having their bachelor and bacherlorette parties after this dinner. Ally's old housekeeper, Mrs. McCarter, had already taken baby Caroline back to Florence Ranch, clearing the way for plenty of fun, although Chet knew that neither Jeremiah nor Ally were going to get too wild.

Yup, Jeremiah's life sure had changed for the better after he'd met his bride.

Once again, Chet's gaze strayed to Mina, as if every cell in his body was drawn to her.

Was there a chance for him, too, if he could just believe that he wouldn't go ruining her life with scandals and a lack of trust that didn't seem to disappear, no matter how hard he tried to banish it?

As if those problems had materialized, the room went a little quieter. Chet guessed the reason before he even saw it.

He'd been waiting all night for Eli Barron to show up.

The older man stood at the fairy-light-lined room entrance, his hat in his hands. Briefly, Chet pictured Eli as the very picture of what he, himself, might resemble in a couple of decades if he kept going down the same road he'd been traveling recently: gray-haired, still stocky but with the slumped shoulders of a beaten man, wrinkle-lined skin, lips in a nervous line as his wary gaze scanned the room.

Always alone, no matter how many people were near him.

Tyler was the first one to go up to his dad, taking the man's hat, welcoming him and sitting him at a table. A waiter came by and Tyler spoke to the man, obviously ordering food for Eli.

Jeremiah said, "I wasn't sure if his ride from the rehab center would get him here on time."

Even so, that was the reason tonight's drinks had been

alcohol free—for Eli's sake. There'd be time enough for carousing after the dinner, at the parties that Eli's curfew kept him from attending.

"I'll bet he busted his ass to make it," Chet said.

"I just hope he lasts through the weekend."

"He's going back Monday, right?"

"Yeah. Tyler said he'd keep a good eye on him, help him to avoid the alcohol that'll be served at the reception. I offered to keep everything dry, but you know how Dad is—he got red in the face and was mortified at even being thought of as the 'head case' who'd put a damper on my big day. I told him it wasn't a problem, that I'd already made plans to have a dry rehearsal dinner here, but he got huffy about how wedding reception plans were much more involved than just some meal's. He said being around regular social scenes would be a good test for him, that he wouldn't be able to ask everyone in the world to stop drinking so he needed to start getting used to being around alcohol now. We've already gotten rid of every bit of it in the mansion though, after last night's cocktail hour."

"So, aside from that, we're all supposed to pretend he's fine? We just go on about our business as if he's not going through rehab?"

"If it makes him feel more empowered in his struggles." Jeremiah paused. "His counselors would like to sit us all down together, just to fill us in on how we should be handling Eli's challenges, too."

"I'll make sure it's a priority." Up until now, Chet had been reading all the literature he could find on how to handle alcoholism.

Jeremiah added, "They'd also like us to look into Al-Anon."

Chet nodded. It wasn't just up to Eli to face his challenges; they'd all have to fight them together.

And, for the first time since the scandal broke, it seemed like everything was falling into place.

Like Jeremiah, Chet put his beer bottle—nonalcoholic of course—on a nearby table.

Eli was still glancing around the room, and when his gaze lit on Chet, it was obvious that he'd been looking for his third son in particular.

A mix of emotions seemed to pass through his eyes: happiness at seeing Chet standing with Jeremiah, embarrassment at having to put his sons through everything they'd endured.

"Here it goes," Jeremiah said, speaking for Chet, too, because they both knew what they needed to do next.

It was just hard to cross the room, say hello, as if everything was wonderful.

Chet felt someone else looking at him from across the way and he knew it was Mina. He met her gaze, inhaled at the zing of it.

One thing was certain—he needed to take care of his relationship with his biological father before he could be good for anyone else.

And when she smiled at him, so comfortingly, so naturally, something lifted within Chet, buoying him, making him think everything *would* be okay because she believed that he could do this.

Chet and Jeremiah made their way through the tables, which had started to clear out after the dinner itself had ended. By the time they got to Eli's table, the waiter had brought a plate of enchiladas, plus rice, beans and tortillas.

Jeremiah took hold of his father's shoulder, squeezing it. "Dad."

It was obvious that they were still working through years of hard times between them, but when Eli reached up to grip Jeremiah's hand, it was enough. Chet could tell by the smile on his brother's face. Even Tyler looked touched as he stood behind Eli's chair.

Eli peered up at Chet, and he saw that his biological father's eyes weren't red with drink. They were clear tonight.

Thank God.

Chet sat in the chair next to Eli. "We were all hoping you'd make it here in time."

And he didn't just mean that it was good to see him at this dinner—it was nice to finally know that Eli had found himself in a better place altogether, in time for his son's wedding.

Finally in the place he needed to be.

"Chet," Eli said, his voice cracking.

Chet glanced at his brothers, and they understood that it was time to leave Eli and his new son alone. That it was time to start the next phase of forgiveness, if they could manage it.

When they were by themselves, Eli spoke first. "How're things at the Utah resort?"

Starting off slow. Okay. That was fine.

"Perfect," Chet said. "No need for you to even think about it."

"I'm retired from the Group now, anyway. But it's tough, after all those years of knowing every detail about every project. I'm sure Tyler feels the same way, now that he's cut himself loose from the Group, too. But it looks like the business is in good hands with you and Jeremiah at the helm."

"It is. You can depend on it."

Eli went quiet, obviously fresh out of the beating-around-the-bush talk.

"Dad," Chet said, hesitantly. "I really am glad you're here."

At the word *Dad,* Eli's head had snapped up. One corner of his mouth twitched, his eyes going hazy.

Chet had never seen Abe, his "other father," cry. He'd been raised to think that men didn't do that.

Just thinking of Abe's lessons made Chet promise that he would remember what his first dad had taught him over the years, even as Chet moved on.

But an emotional snag remained. By forgiving Eli, would he be trading one father for another? Was he spitting on the memory of the man who'd raised him?

Brushing that aside for now, he put his hand on Eli's forearm, and the older man's eyes welled up as Chet's own gaze went bleary.

Mina left the restaurant with Ally, Zoe and Ally's aunt Jessica, but she didn't say goodbye to Chet. He was still with his biological father, and it was clear that they shouldn't be interrupted.

And that was the best news Mina could've imagined.

She couldn't stop smiling, even though there was a scratching in her throat that brought a little happiness/sadness to the sensation.

"Mina," Ally said in her refined, gentle voice as they got to the limo parked in front of their restaurant. "Are you all right?"

"Yeah. It's just the whole business with Eli..."

Aunt Jessica, a spitfire forty-year-old who looked more like a carefree thirty-year-old, put a hand over Mina's mouth. "Not tonight, okay? Y'all can talk about maudlin matters after we've drank and danced and made a bride-to-be fool out of Ally, and not a minute before."

Zoe laughed as they climbed into the limo. "Sensitive as always, Jess."

Jessica tossed back a lock of her sun-kissed brunette hair. "Honey, I'm the party mistress, and I take my task quite seriously."

"Yes, ma'am." Ally saluted.

But she wasn't so obedient when Jess pulled out a bag from under a limo seat, giving her niece a sparkly princess crown, a sash that read, "Kiss me!" and a glowing green wand.

Ally's crown was crooked as she sat back in the seat and the limo pulled forward. "This is degrading, Jess."

Zoe and Mina couldn't hold back a spate of giggles. So wrong to laugh, but Mina couldn't stop herself. She was absolutely giddy—for Ally, for Jeremiah, for Chet and his dad.

And for the baby who would soon be announced to his or her father, now that it seemed things were on track.

Jess broke out some champagne. "Drink up, my darlings."

Of course, Mina declined any.

Ally sat there holding her silly wand. "Where're you taking us, Jess?"

"Yeah," Zoe said. "It's not like Duarte Hill is the party spot of the millennium."

"Well, girls," Jess said, "you know I like to wing it, but this time I did my homework. If you'd done yours, you'd know that there's a social dance about two miles down a country lane off the main road in a community hall. I'm betting there'll be a buffet of cowboys there."

"Cowboys?" Ally asked. "I'm already getting married to one. Tomorrow, if you'll recall."

"Who said the cowboys are for you?" Jess asked.

Soon they pulled up to a building that resembled an old wood warehouse, with weathered gray walls and light peeking out from the slats of wood. Country music from a live band blared out.

"Yee-haw," Jess said, the first one out of the limo.

Zoe adjusted Ally's crown, then made her take off the "Kiss me!" sash, much to Ally's relief.

"Good call," Mina said. "I could just see that thing causing a lot of trouble." It would be bad enough that Ally was gorgeous and would attract every cowboy's stare within gaping distance.

Inside, streamers hung from the rafters; the smell of old hay, along with that of hops, was woven through the body-warmed air. All around them there were indeed cowboys, but there were a good many cowgirls, too, wearing tight jeans and curious looks as the bachelorette party strolled inside with Princess Ally and her glowing horny-green wand.

Mina and Zoe flanked the bride-to-be.

"Don't worry," Zoe yelled over the music. "We'll protect you."

But then Jess came over to pull Ally away, toward

a corner where a keg stood, surrounded by young, strapping ranch hands.

Zoe shrugged and said in Mina's ear, "Jess is harmless. She won't let anybody get near Ally." She nodded toward the keg. "I need some of that beer."

"Party away."

Zoe left, and within ten minutes, all of them were on the dance floor, whooping it up, fending off the cowboys, who joined in the whole bachelorette party fervor with friendly abandon.

They danced and danced—swinging, line dancing—and all the while, Mina imagined that every partner was really Chet. After a while though, the fantasy chipped away at her, because she realized that there would never be another man who would live up to him.

She *had* to tell him everything this weekend. Holding it in was breaking her down, day by day. And it just didn't seem fair to him, either, because what if the news actually brought him further along in his healing?

Then again, what if it didn't...?

As a swing dance ended and everyone applauded, the cowboy Mina had been dancing with bowed to her and went off to grab a drink, clearly sensing that he wasn't going to get anywhere with Mina tonight.

That was when a loud "Whoo-hoo!" broke the atmosphere.

Mina whipped her gaze to the building's entrance, where Jeremiah Barron was waving his hat.

Then he headed straight over to Ally, who jumped into his arms just before he swung her around.

Zoe rushed to Tyler, too, and he dipped her back in a long kiss that made a few of the nearby cowboys and girls hoot.

Then came the one man Mina had been hoping to see.

Chet sauntered over to her, tipping back his cowboy hat, revealing a tuft of his dark blond hair. Judging from the wide smile on him, things had gone well with Eli.

Her pulse gave a big bang.

The band hadn't started a new song yet, so she had no problems hearing him when he said, "Jess told Jeremiah where you girls were heading."

"Thank goodness. I was looking for a dance partner who could keep up with me."

Boy—for a woman who'd been playing her cards close to her chest ever since she and Chet had left the resort, her statement seemed pretty bold.

The band launched into a song that begged for a two-step.

Chet looked like he'd just come off of the range in his jeans and cowboy gear, but when he took Mina into his arms, it was as if the gentlemanly side of him—the part that was perfectly comfortable in a designer business suit—had come out to take over.

He eased her into the flowing dance, his mouth near her ear. Mina shivered as her temple brushed the five o'clock shadow on his cheek. His clover-and-hay smell sent her reeling.

She whispered, "So everything's okay?"

He knew that she was asking about him and his dad. "Eli and I are going to settle in for a longer talk tomorrow, before the wedding. His driver had to get him back to the mansion early. A curfew is a condition of this weekend pass from rehab."

Content, she rested her head on his shoulder.

He gripped her hand in his, tightening his hold on her hip, too. Her breathing spiked as heat banded every inch of her.

They weren't doing the two-step anymore—they were lost in their own world instead. Through her lashes, she could see the cowboys and girls on the edges of the dance floor, watching them. It was mainly the women who had such poignant looks on their faces—the type Mina knew she used to wear whenever she would think about Chet, longing for him, wondering if her love for him would ever be noticed or come to fruition.

Then she saw Ally and Jeremiah on the dance floor, holding each other, too. As the bride-to-be met Mina's gaze, she smiled, one woman in love to another.

A couple. Everyone seemed to be thinking that Mina and Chet were together, and she wanted to believe that with all of her soul.

She never wanted this dance to end, even as the notes swayed toward their inevitable finale, the music swelling, then fading off as everyone clapped.

As the band switched to a fast song, Mina glanced up at Chet, drawing away from him ever so slightly. They were still holding each other, as if he was just as unwilling to let go.

But their connection was broken when Tyler passed by, nudging Chet.

It only took an instant for Mina to see the reason.

Jeremiah was at the keg, and so was Eli.

Mina did a double take.

Eli?

Tyler joined his brother and dad, just as Chet cursed over the music, then headed over there, too, Mina's heart going with him.

* * *

Jeremiah's voice belted over the music as he burned a stare through Eli but addressed his brothers instead.

"Dad tells me that he wasn't intending to get himself any beer. He was just standing here, watching the party."

"It's true," Eli said, his aged skin going ruddy. "I wasn't going to pour myself a drink."

Tyler asked, "Then why were you standing by a keg, Dad?"

"I was just walking by. You have to believe me."

Whether or not he was lying, Chet had heard this all before. So had Tyler and Jeremiah. And they knew that when Eli got called out and felt backed into a corner, it never turned out well.

And he'd thought tonight was a turning point.

Chet said, "You're supposed to be in bed by now. That's what you told me back at the restaurant."

That stubborn bull-about-to-charge intensity heated up Eli's gaze. "I just wanted to come here and be with my family for a short time. Is that too much to ask?"

Tyler grit his teeth. "Is it too much to ask for you to stick to your guns, Dad? You were doing so well at rehab."

"And I'm still doing well, Ty." He took off his hat, jutted out his chin. "Want to smell my breath to see if there's any alcohol on it? Go ahead."

They all glanced at the beer keg, where a ranch hand was watching them from beneath the brim of his hat while pouring himself a cup.

Chet couldn't stand this farce anymore, and he took his dad by the shirtsleeve, thinking it'd be a good idea to get him away from temptation.

Eli resisted. "Hey—"

His face was so red that Chet let go of his shirt. He noticed that Mina had followed him over here, and she looked more devastated than he felt.

But why, when *he* was the one whose world was crashing, just when he thought it'd gone upright again?

Eli was breathing in and out, and Chet wondered if that's what they'd taught him at rehab—exercises to calm himself.

Finally, he said, "I'm not a child who needs babysitting."

Tyler shot another emphatic glance at the keg, expressing his doubt. Jeremiah just stared at the floor, shaking his head.

Eli looked to Chet, as if his third son was the only one who might believe him, even though he'd been the toughest one to win over.

"I'm telling the truth. You believe me, don't you?"

Truth. Chet wanted to ask him the definition of it, because it sure seemed to be a different matter to the man who called himself his father.

Eli apparently lost all the fight he had left in him, his shoulders slumping again as he straightened his jacket, then his bolo, mustering his dignity.

It was those little gestures that made Chet think that maybe there *was* hope for Eli yet. That all he'd wanted to do was be near the son who was getting married tomorrow, to take part in a bit of the happiness the rest of the family was experiencing.

The music cut off just before Eli said, "Forgive me for ruining your night. Forgive me for everything."

With that, he headed toward the exit. None of the brothers stopped him.

Chet looked to Mina, who'd always been the calm in his every storm.

But when he saw the sympathy and sorrow in her gaze, his heart sank to the bottom of his chest, where it always seemed to land.

Chapter Nine

The party had lost its air after Eli had gone home, and the brothers had decided to return to Florence Ranch, too.

Mina had left with the women in the limo. The only one of them who'd had any remaining will to celebrate was Jess, and she'd agreed to put an end to the evening when she'd heard about Eli's appearance.

Mina had gone back to her guest cottage, not expecting to see any more of Chet tonight, even after that dance they'd shared. That magical moment that hadn't lasted nearly as long as she would've liked.

It was morning when she saw him again.

She was strolling out in the gardens in back of the mansion with Caroline, Ally's baby daughter. Since the bride had a mile-long list of things to do today, along with her maids of honor Mrs. McCarter and Jess, Mina had volunteered to switch off with Zoe in watching over the child.

They were walking down one of the gravel maze paths amidst the roses, but Mina didn't see many of them. Caroline's little pink face, which was peeking out from under her knit cap and her swaddling blanket, outshone all the flowers.

Is my baby going to be a sweet little girl like you? Mina thought, brushing a finger down Caroline's soft cheek. *Or am I going to have a boy who turns out to be as big and strong as his daddy?*

Caroline smiled up at her, and Mina bit her lip. She wished she'd asked the doctor about her baby's sex.

She became aware that she wasn't alone when she heard the crunch of boots over the gravel. Looking up, she saw Chet, his hat in his hands, a mysterious slant to his gaze that seemed full of questions.

But there was a gentleness there, too.

He put his hat back on his head, as if that would cover what she'd seen in him, but she remembered anyway. Her heart had stamped his gaze all over the inside of her chest.

"I thought I should come out here and fetch you for breakfast," he said. "It'll be ready in about fifteen minutes in the smaller dining room."

"The smaller dining room as opposed to the big one, huh? Imagine living in a house with a choice of either."

"I don't really live here." He knit his brow, then gestured toward the house. "It's buffet style, so no hurry. No fuss."

Mina smiled. "Somehow, I don't associate the term *no fuss* with Florence Ranch."

"I never did, either—not until I got to know Tyler and Jeremiah better. They're different than when they were young, when I would come here to visit. They used to be boarding school rich kids." His own smile held a touch of wistfulness. "Abe didn't believe in sending me away for my education. He and Mom kept me at home."

"Seems to have worked out just fine for you."

A loaded pause balanced between them.

He broke it, looking at the baby, then coming toward her and Caroline, who locked her gaze onto him, enthralled.

"Look at that," Mina said. "She likes you."

"Maybe because I resemble Jeremiah a bit." He touched the baby's bunched hand. "I'm not used to being around children, but since I'm going to be an uncle, I supposed I'd better get used to it."

You're going to be more than an uncle, she thought. But then she recalled how coiled he'd seemed last night, after he and his brothers had confronted Eli at that dance.

More time. He just needed a little more time to come around, and then…

"Here you go," she said, handing Caroline to him, a lump in her throat.

Without hesitation, Chet took the baby into his arms. A natural, just as he'd been when he'd taken his place at the Barron Group.

It occurred to Mina that he was the type of man who might be good at just about everything, although he didn't make a show of it.

Would he be just as natural a father?

He was still pretty quiet, and she suspected he was waiting to say something, probably about the awkwardness of last night with Eli. It would be just like Chet to apologize for the situation, which had been out of his control.

Finally, he spoke. "You should see Jeremiah. He's fit to jump out of his skin right about now."

Not what she'd been expecting him to say. Maybe he was working his way around to it, as always.

"The former playboy's getting cold feet?" Mina asked.

"I think he just wants to get all the ceremonial stuff over with and be with his family in peace." Chet was grinning down at Caroline, and the baby was still enamored of him.

"Ally's as cool as ever," Mina said. "I was with her first thing this morning, checking to see if she needed anything."

"I have no doubt you were of great help."

He transferred that adoring smile to Mina, and she just about melted, even though he was talking about one of her sore points—her propensity to be such a people pleaser.

Then it hit her: had she been doing her best to please Chet, too, just like anyone else?

The more she thought about it, the more it seemed like a real possibility. She'd been dancing around him with the paternity situation, putting all the pressure on herself without seriously giving him the benefit of the doubt when it came to taking the news well.

Had she taken her neuroses too far? Was this more about *her* than *him?*

While she was mulling over that, Chet had taken to rocking the baby ever so slightly, and Caroline's eyes were beginning to close, little flutters of sleepiness.

The movement echoed in Mina's chest, and she struggled to maintain herself.

She started up the conversation again. "Ally's going to be such a beautiful bride."

Now she sounded downright yearning, and Chet looked up from the baby, noticing it, as well.

"Don't they say that every bride is beautiful?" he asked.

"Some more than others, I suspect."

"Well, I'll tell you what—you'll be outshining everyone in that ballroom today, Mina."

The sincerity of his tone bowled her over, weakening her in the knees and threatening to take her down.

The atmosphere had changed between them, going from tense to absolutely laden, weighed with things they couldn't, *wouldn't,* talk about.

"Mina," he said, "I owe you a long talk. As much as I'm ashamed to say it, I've been putting it off, just like I put off making my peace with Eli for so long."

She got the bad feeling that she was someone to "make peace with," too, and that didn't sit well.

Was he going to tell her that a romantic relationship just wasn't going to work out, even before she told him what *he* needed to know?

All of a sudden, it was as if she was hearing her drunken uncle at that barbecue all those years ago, and he was spouting another truth, this time directly to her.

No one wants you, Mina. You're an accident to everyone.

Her world spun, nightmarishly fast—images of her raising the baby alone or, worse yet, her having to trade off with Chet for visitation...

Before she could ask Chet to come out with what was in his heart, footsteps sounded on the path.

Mina turned to find Zoe rounding a tall hedge. Her dark shoulder-length hair was cut straight, and it swung with every step.

"Hi, there," she said, giving Mina and Chet the same glance from last night, when they'd been slow dancing like a real couple.

After Mina and Chet quietly greeted her, Zoe held out her arms for the sleeping Caroline.

"I grabbed some breakfast early," she said, "so I'm free to steal the baby while you take care of yourself, Mina."

Chet gave the precious cargo to Zoe, who shot a sympathetic glance to him.

"Chet," she said, "Eli's on the patio. He's been asking where you are."

"Thanks, Zoe."

She left Chet and Mina standing there, his hands in his jeans pockets, her arms crossed over her chest.

"You should go to him," Mina said, almost relieved that she and Chet wouldn't be able to talk until after the wedding. She was so afraid of what he might say… and about how this conversation with his father might ultimately affect everything.

"I'll see you at the wedding," Chet said, but he seemed hesitant to leave.

So she deserted him first, just as she might have to do anyway.

Chet kept thinking that there was something that he should go back and say to Mina before he went to his father, but he wasn't sure what it was.

I'm sorry for always having to leave you hanging?

I'm sorry my life is such a mess that it doesn't leave all that much time for you?

As he rounded the tall hedges and spotted his father standing on the patio in front of the French doors, a glass of what looked to be orange juice on the table near him, Chet fisted his hands by his sides.

He was sick of apologizing to Mina—just as sick as she must've been in hearing him. He was sick of how his life had spun out of control and he'd been too stubborn and angry to get a grip on it.

Most of all, he was sick of how Eli tested them, over and over again.

When the old man heard him coming, he forced a smile that seemed to wobble in its uncertainty. He also noticed how Chet gave a pointed glance to that orange juice glass.

"Nothing toxic mixed in," Eli said, picking up the drink and offering it to Chet so he could sample it.

Chet held up his hand. "No, thanks."

"I just thought that maybe, after last night…"

"You already told us that you weren't near that keg to nip a drink."

"Yes, I did. But what matters is that I think you still don't believe me."

Chet wanted to. Lord, did he ever.

Eli sank to a stone bench, which sat near an empty fountain, sapped of water.

"To tell you the truth," he said, "I'm not sure what the hell I was doing. One minute I was walking into that dance, the next I was by that keg." His face was ruddy again, but not from anger. "Maybe you boys saved me just in time. I don't know. It might've only taken a few more seconds before that beer was really calling to me."

His candidness struck Chet.

Eli continued talking. "I'm going to go back to rehab tonight, and I'm going to make every one of you proud. Before I leave though..." He put down his juice. "Chet, I'm not asking for you to really think of me as your father... But I'd like you to know that I love you just as much as I can love any son."

Chet mulled that over for a second, a sense of wrongness creeping up on him until he understood just what it meant.

He sat down on the bench, too, but there was still a space between him and Eli. "One reason that I've had such a hard time coming to terms with you is that I feel like accepting you is a betrayal of Abe."

"He wouldn't feel that way, Chet."

"That could very well be. But Abe was the victim in all this, and the last thing I'd ever do is stop backing him up, even if he's gone now. Abe and I had our tough times when I went off to Montana, but I *never* fully turned my back on him. To do it now is...unthinkable."

Eli apparently knew better than to offer his own opinion. But, then again, he knew Chet pretty well, because when he'd first moved down to Texas, Eli had been the first to welcome him home, the first to seemingly understand him. He'd been every nephew's dream of an uncle until he'd turned out to be something else altogether.

"I think," Chet said, his tone lowered, pained, "that when I left my parents all those years ago, I might've done it for more reasons than just wanting to experience some freedom. There was always something unspoken between my parents, and now that I know what it was,

I wonder if *that* was why I wanted to go. So I wouldn't have to endure those looks between them anymore." He shook his head. "Even then, I knew there were lies going on, and it's the lies that have bothered me the most about any of this."

And he couldn't stand any more of them. They'd nearly ruined so many people around him.

"I did the most lying, Chet," his dad said. "You need to put the blame squarely on me."

"Don't forget my mom."

"She was saving her marriage. I kept my silence so I could maintain my marriage, too, but…" Eli wilted a little. "I was also doing it so I could save face. Your mom didn't care about that as much as she cared about you and Abe."

When Chet looked into his father's eyes, he knew that Eli meant everything he was saying.

And, the thing was, they were the same eyes that Abe had: blue, forthright, clear as a Texas sky now that Eli was sober.

"I'm not going to put anything on you," Chet said. "Not anymore. You need to know that, and I should've been able to say it sooner. Resentment hasn't gotten me anywhere."

"Stop it, Chet. You have nothing to apologize for, especially after going through the scandal, then…"

Eli choked to a halt, and Chet knew why. He had the same rock in his throat that the other man probably did.

Abe's death.

Would the grief ever stop? It'd gotten buried these past months, a dusting of ground over the agony, a shallow grave where Chet had stored his sadness.

But what kept him from fully turning away from that grave was that he'd never gotten to know Abe as well as he could've as an adult. *He'd* been the one who'd blown that chance when he'd left his family behind, going off to Montana, telling his father he didn't want to be cooped up in an office.

Utterly leaving him until the cancer had come.

How could he get over that? When?

What scared Chet was there was even a chance that, if he didn't help Eli to bury his *own* sorrows, he would suffer from even more regret someday. He would've denied yet another father.

So cowboy up then, he thought. *Onward.*

But the last word made him think of Mina.

Was he ready to go onward, forward, clear to move ahead with everything he'd been denying himself with her?

He glanced at his dad. No more regrets.

Onward. With *everyone.*

Feeling as if he had shed about a hundred pounds, Chet took up where he and Eli had left off yesterday at the rehearsal dinner, before they'd had that setback at the party.

He rested his hand on his father's shoulder, neither of them needing to say much more as, in the distance, from the ballroom, the notes from the band rehearsing the wedding music floated through the air, celebrating today's unions and reunions.

The minute Mina saw Chet walk into the wedding, she knew everything had changed for the better.

As he came down the red-carpeted aisle behind Tyler and Jeremiah, he was all shined up, his normally tousled dark blond hair combed back to go along with the black suit he wore as one of the best men. When he caught her eye from his place by his brother near the altar, he gave her such a dazzling smile that her head whirled.

Whatever had gone on between him and Eli this morning, it'd been life altering.

Her pulse started bopping, and she hugged her hands over her belly.

The small orchestra, composed of three violins, a cello and a harp, played Bach while everyone got settled under the golden chandeliers. Outside the large French doors, the gardens bloomed under an overcast sky.

Eli came down the aisle next, dressed in a tuxedo with a bolo, and he and all the Barron boys exchanged a long glance before the older man took his seat in the front row.

Maybe it was pregnancy hormones, but Mina got the sudden urge to cry. She held it back magnificently until she realized that there were no more parents coming down the aisle because the bride's mom and dad had died, so there was no one to give Ally away.

It made Mina think of her baby and what it would be like to miss her own son or daughter's wedding because of a tragedy.

But she was being dramatic, maudlin.

Definitely pregnancy hormones.

Zoe, dressed in a blue sheath dress, slid into the seat next to Mina's. She was holding Caroline, who was making little sucking noises while swathed in her blanket.

"Just in the nick of time," she whispered as the symphony struck the first chords of the "Bridal March."

The small crowd, mainly consisting of Ally and Jeremiah's friends, plus a few work associates, stood, facing the back of the ballroom.

Ally entered, breathtaking in her Jackie O.–inspired gown, her platinum hair twisted into a classic upsweep. Her old housekeeper, Mrs. McCarter, was dolled up, too, wearing a sage satin dress with a matching cashmere sweater while using her cane to walk with Ally down the aisle. Mina realized that the elderly woman was the one who was giving Ally away to the groom, and that brought on the tears again. Ally had told Mina last night how Mrs. McCarter had just about raised her as the household manager for her parents. Even after they'd died, she'd been there through thick and thin, the closest thing Ally had to a family now.

Behind them, Ally's aunt Jess wore the same dress as Mrs. McCarter, but without the sweater. They were all gorgeous, and Mina couldn't help wishing that she and Chet…

No. She wouldn't get ahead of herself. Not before she could have that heart-to-heart with him.

When Mina saw how Jeremiah's love shone in his gaze as he watched Ally come to the altar, tears leaked out of Mina's eyes.

But then she looked at Chet, who was watching *her.*

And he seemed just as smitten with Mina as she'd always been with him.

She drew in a breath just as the preacher asked everyone to be seated.

Don't sob, she thought. *No matter how happy you are, don't do it....*

She managed to hold it back to mere tears as the ceremony went by in a stream of color and longing.

Afterward, the wedding party had to duck out for pictures, trying Mina's patience.

As she sat at the bridal party's table in a Victorian-wallpapered formal dining room that was even larger than the regular one, Zoe took a chair next to her. The other woman had gone up to Ally's room to put a tuckered Caroline to sleep, and a babysitter would be watching over the baby until the reception ended and Zoe could take over again, leaving Ally and Jeremiah to their honeymoon night.

Zoe sipped from a glass of sparkling water garnished with lime, inspecting Mina, who tried to seem as if she wasn't wishing for a certain cowboy to walk through the door.

Then she put down her glass. "He's probably just as anxious about getting those photos over with as you are."

Mina tried to play innocent, cocking her eyebrow. *Whoever are you talking about?*

Zoe just laughed. "Yeah. I haven't noticed how you and Chet are mooning over each other at all. And it can't be easy on your part, with all the Greek tragedy going on in this family."

Nailed.

Zoe continued. "Take a word of advice from someone who knows what it's like to fall for a Barron—just be patient. Things will calm down and life will go on. Tyler was just as angry and confused as Chet when the scandal first broke, and I swear, he was like a..." She smiled, as if deep in memory. "Well, like a horse that had to be gentled."

"I've been trying to hang in there." Mina smiled. "I'd do anything for him."

She might've been embarrassed to tell that to anyone else—to lay out her heart so thoroughly. But Zoe had gone through this, too. She'd been the PR rep who'd controlled the Barron scandal, but then she'd become so much more to Tyler.

The other woman said, "Even Ty knew what's been going on between you two a long time ago."

Mina stopped reaching for her water glass. Had Chet told his brother that he'd ended up in Mina's bed the night he'd heard about his parentage?

But Zoe put her fears to rest when she said, "It was in the way Chet acted around you at our wedding. The way Chet would light up whenever you called him on the phone. Not too hard to miss, even if you're an alpha male who refuses to even watch a romantic comedy with his wife."

Mina allowed herself to relax. Maybe no one knew just how far things had gone with her and Chet.

It wasn't long before the bridal party entered the room to much applause and toasts. But nothing else seemed to exist as Chet headed straight for the bridal party's table.

To Mina.

Her heart stuttered as she caught scent of him—the clover, the hay, the way no one else smelled and appealed to her.

When he took her hand under the table and squeezed it, she nearly flew with absolute joy.

A smile curved his mouth, and she didn't have to ask about how this latest talk had gone with Eli.

And when he leaned toward her to whisper in her ear, she closed her eyes, thinking that she'd never felt so dizzy, so in love.

"Let's scram as soon as we can."

She nodded, unable to speak.

She would be doing enough talking soon, when they were alone and she dropped her wonderful bombshell on him.

Chapter Ten

It seemed as if time trudged by during the reception, but Chet was going to make the most of it, dancing the hours away with Mina until they could escape.

Until they could finally be alone, now that he'd cleared some of the webs from his life.

But by the time the bride and groom were ready to cut their wedding cake, Chet was done waiting.

Most of the guests were on the temporary dance floor that was surrounded by the dining tables; everyone was standing in front of the tall, white layered cake, complete with a bride and cowboy groom at the top of it.

Chet leaned down to Mina, brushing back her hair from her ear, whispering into it.

"Are you ready to scoot?"

She smiled, and when she looked into his eyes, it seemed that she reached right into him and pulled out everything he had, heart and soul.

His pulse sped up, and, in the back of his mind, he experienced everything around him going faster, faster than ever before.

The ink isn't even dry on your new lease on life with Eli, yet here you are rushing headlong into a relationship with Mina?

But from the way he ached as she slid her hand into his, he knew that it was way past time.

Everyone cheered while Jeremiah and Ally fed each other the cake slices. Meanwhile, Mina whispered into Chet's ear.

"Why don't you grab a couple of plates and meet me at my cottage?"

Again, there was that out-of-control merry-go-round sensation of speed, of going too damned fast.

But he ignored it. "Will do."

As the band began to play, the crowd started dancing again, this time to some awful yet peppy chicken song.

Mina slipped out of the throng, toward the exit, virtually unnoticed. Chet watched her, wearing his heart on his jacket sleeve.

The way she looked in that bronze-colored dress, which rivaled her hair in color and shine...the way the silk draped over her hips as she swayed out the door...

She really was the most stunning woman in the room, just as he had told her she would be. He doubted he would ever find another person as beautiful, inside and out.

Feeling more light-headed than ever, Chet casually grabbed two slices of cake from the tray of a passing waiter, who was depositing the desserts at each place setting. Then he stealthily made his way out of the room, the weird chicken music left behind him.

Perfect time to get going.

He made his way through the big house, out a side door, then took a path toward the nearby guest cottage with soft light burning through the windows.

He managed to knock, even with two fistfuls of plate.

When Mina opened the door, the dim illumination shone from behind her, creating an aura that kissed every strand of gold in her red hair. She'd already kicked off her shoes, revealing scarlet-tipped toenails, and already taken off the wrap that had draped over her shoulders and arms. But she still wore that dress, and it fell nearly to her feet like a shower of bronze.

"I thought you'd never get here with my sugar fix," she said, taking the plates from him. "I've been craving cake all day."

As he came inside, he thought that she might've had a slight tremor in her voice, even though she was smiling.

Nerves?

He wasn't sure why she would be anxious around him, unless it was just the anticipation of what this night might bring.

But what was *that* exactly?

What was he expecting—for them to make love again? Or did he want much, much more this soon?

Again, his pulse raced.

If she didn't have nerves, he definitely did.

He shut the door behind him while she headed for the small kitchen, with its square wooden table smack in the middle of the tiled flooring. Coffee was brewing in a machine on the counter, and she'd lit a couple of candles. That plus a lantern hanging over the stove provided the only light in the area.

She set the plates on the table, then laughed.

"What?" he asked.

"I just realized...I think I've recreated that scene from *Sixteen Candles.* You know—the ending, where Molly Ringwald is celebrating her birthday with her dream guy?"

Dream guy.

There was a lot of pressure in that description, if Mina was indeed comparing him to the hero of the movie.

Adrenaline spun through him, but he told himself that they'd been heading to this point the entire time they'd known each other.

And it *wasn't* too soon.

"Sorry," he said. "That kind of movie really isn't my thing. I haven't seen it."

"It's a great one." Was she talking faster than usual? "Everyone around Molly has forgotten her sixteenth birthday. They're rushing all over the place, paying attention to other matters, like her sister's wedding. But she finally gets what she wants in the end."

Okay. He understood why the movie might've been significant to Mina, with how she'd felt about being an accidental baby, forgotten herself sometimes.

But she'd chosen *him* to make her feel special, just like the heroine in that movie had been with her dream man.

Mina had already put forks and napkins by the plates, and now she was pouring water into tall glasses. Putting down the pitcher, she blew out a breath, smoothed out her dress.

Everything was feeling real innocent right about now, as if it was the first time he'd been alone with her, boy with girl.

Man with woman.

Coming up behind her, he rested his hands on her arms. He felt her shiver.

But the same was happening to him—washes of desire traveling his skin, cool and warm at the same time.

He leaned down, his face against her hair. The scent of her—cucumber, green tea… Heady and clean.

"I can't tell you how it feels to finally be away from everyone else," he said. "Every*thing* else."

"Why don't you try to tell me, anyway?"

He ran his hands down her bare arms, and she crossed them over her chest until he was embracing her from the back.

"Freedom," he said. "It was like I was locked up and then let out. That's how it felt with all those lies—like they were pushing me back and keeping me from going anywhere. But they've all been cleared up now with Eli."

"Everything's in the clear?" she asked.

"Yeah." He tightened his hold on her, releasing a little when he realized he might be overdoing it. "I swear, if I'd had to deal with one more lie…"

She stiffened beneath him.

He thought he could feel the beat of her pulse under his own skin, a skittering rhythm. Or maybe it was just her breathing, faster now.

Was she afraid that he would never fully pull himself

out of his family drama? That the fallout from the scandal was going to linger and affect *them?*

"There won't be anything else coming between us," he said. "Don't worry about that."

"At least you've learned how to handle it when someone hasn't been entirely truthful with you," she said, her words seeming...careful. Very careful. "Did you get any perspective on why other people might've had to pull back on telling you the truth? I know what your mom and Eli did wasn't right, but..." She turned her head just a tad, still not looking at him. "Can you understand, even a shred, why they might've kept you in the dark?"

"I've tried. But it all keeps boiling down to this—Eli and my mom could've avoided hurting a lot of people if they'd come clean a lot earlier." He shook his head. "There's never a good enough reason to hide the truth."

"Never?"

She still sounded odd, but he couldn't read her face since she'd turned away from him again.

He eased her around so he could see her. "None of that matters now. Eli and I are starting up a new relationship." Even as he said it, there was something dragging at him—the truth of how he still felt. "Okay, maybe there's always going to be a part of me that remembers how he held back the truth for so many years. Same with my mom. But, with her, I'll never have the opportunity to tell her how much damage she did."

"I wish she was here, and not just so you could straighten matters out with her, too," Mina said.

He hugged her to him. Mina, his saving grace, the woman who always seemed to keep him balanced.

"I'm still angry at her," he said. "And if you hadn't come into my life, I even wonder if I might've ended up with a woman who would lie to me like my mom did to Abe at first. How's that for some neuroses?"

"You can't generalize like that, Chet."

Then she fell silent.

He kissed her head, wanting her to know that everything would improve from this night on.

"You're right—I shouldn't generalize," he said. "You're the most trustworthy person I know."

She was gripping his hand now, finally looking at him, but with a hint of anxiety in her gaze.

He strove to reassure her. "I was so afraid of bringing you into my life. My God, what woman in her right mind would ask to be a part of it?"

"I've told you before—I was always determined to be there for you throughout everything, thick and thin. All I've ever wanted was to see you heal up…"

Touched, he pulled out a kitchen chair, sat down on it, bringing her onto his lap. She snuggled against him, her face near his neck, her hair brushing his skin and driving him crazy. When she spoke, her breath tickled him.

"Everything I've ever done," she said softly, "it's been because I was thinking about what might be best for you."

"I know." He kissed her temple. "Because you're my girl."

It was as if that particular sentiment had twisted something within her, and she pressed her face against him harder.

He felt wet skin. Tears?

Leaning back, he cupped a hand under her jaw. "Why are you crying?"

She seemed on the edge of saying something, but then shook her head.

Why was she so sad when this should be the happiest moment of their lives?

All he wanted to do was bring her to where he was—happy. Finally happy.

He pressed his mouth to hers, tenderly, with all the affection he'd been fighting before now.

"I love you, Mina," he said.

They were the words she'd been hoping for, but she barely registered them through all the confused feelings that were tearing her up: wanting to love him right back, needing to tell him that maybe he wouldn't feel so kindly toward her after she revealed that she, too, was a liar.

But there'd been such good reasons for not telling him about their own big, life-altering news.

Would it be too late to explain that to him? Or was he going to put her in the same category as his mother, whom he obviously hadn't come to terms with yet?

Damn the woman for never telling Chet the truth. Yet Mina couldn't be angry at a ghost, not when there was a man, flesh and blood, looking down at her with such openness and hope in his blue gaze.

Her instincts told her to just show him that she would *always* be his, no matter what she'd done to him.

"I love you, too," she said, sadness making the words raw in her throat. "I love you so much, Chet."

His smile was so beautiful—relaying what no other words could've possibly accomplished—that it was beyond Mina to tell him to wait and hear her out.

Before she could say anything else, he kissed her, and it was everything to her—full of the true affection he'd never admitted before now, full of the unconditional love she'd been searching for all her life.

She wasn't a mistake to him, not this time.

Not until the truth would destroy everything she'd labored so hard to build with him. And she couldn't stand to injure him again, not after he'd finally found a measure of peace tonight.

She kissed him back with everything she had in her—months of watching him from afar, of having to keep a yearning distance between them at work. Surely she could hold on to this complete and utter happiness just a little longer....

Groaning low in his throat, he slowed the kiss down, gently nipping at her, weaving his fingers through her hair in a lazy exploration that sent waves of heat through her. Her blood pounded, marching toward the low center of her body, where it gathered, demanding.

"Mina," he said against her lips, and she couldn't let go of how that made her feel—as if she was wanted more than any woman could've ever felt wanted.

As he held her on his lap, brushing her hair back from her face, she saw in those eyes how much he did love her, had maybe always loved her.

He leaned over and blew out the candles on the table, one, then the other.

She longed for him to kiss her again, but he took her by the hand instead, leading her to the lantern over the stove. He doused that, too, then brought her to her bedroom, where moonlight rolled through the open curtains at her window.

Around them, the sunrise paintings breathed soft,

dim hues, the splash of them echoing inside of her, coloring her with a desire so strong that she could barely stand it.

His whisper dominated the semidarkness. "I'm never going to let you down again, Mina. I'm going to make up for all the times I disappointed you, starting now."

But *she* was going to disappoint *him,* and it seemed inevitable, even now, when she was trying so hard to show him that she hadn't meant to lie—had only had his best interests at heart…

An ache split her, and it had nothing to do with her desire for him. It started in her chest, as if prying her apart in two directions.

Was he going to call her a liar when she revealed the baby to him? Was he going to put everything in generalities again and tell her that, even though she'd only been looking out for him, there was no reason to ever keep such important news from someone you loved?

He ran his hands down her arms, up again, as if memorizing every inch of her. Then, with deliberation, he reached to the back of her dress, looking for a zipper.

Not finding it there, he skimmed a hand to her side, discovering it, laughing low—an intimate laugh that made her turn fluid.

He unzipped that dress, and the sound resembled what he was doing to her, too: dividing her, taking her apart.

As he peeled the material away from her torso, she churned with need, not only because of the air hitting her bared skin, but because she was getting more and more revealed, even if her body didn't scream "pregnant!" just yet.

Still, she didn't know what to do—stop him?

No. She wanted to keep going. Oh, she wanted it so badly.

Couldn't she just tell him everything after they made love?

Definitely. She would definitely do it then, in the afterglow, when the news couldn't be anything but beautiful and right.

Leaving her dress bunched at her hips, he coaxed off her bra. She didn't have the willpower to put a halt to it.

And when his hungry gaze devoured her exposed breasts, she felt such a rush of emotion for him that she couldn't do anything more than give in all the way.

Then he turned her around, her bare back to his chest. Cupping her breasts, he rubbed her with his thumbs, bringing her to even harder peaks.

She wanted to cry out, but all she could do was make little sounds of utter enjoyment.

"I love every curve of you," he said. "Every inch."

He kissed her neck and she shivered.

After he backed away from her for a moment, she heard the rustle of clothing, the crinkle of packaging.

It didn't take but a minute for him to return, and this time he was naked, except for a condom that he must've gotten from his wallet. She could feel him against her, hard and ready.

And she was as lost as lost could be.

He pushed her hair aside, kissed the bump on the back of her neck, then trailed down her spine, planting another kiss. Another.

"I love," he said, his hands braced on her material-shrouded hips, "the dimples you have just above your derriere."

Gasping, she thought just how much she wanted to worship him, too.

To show him how she would always be devoted to him, no matter what.

She turned around, pulling him up to a stand, then pushed him toward the bed. He fell back onto it, all muscled male beauty on the light field of her covers.

"I love so many things about you, too," she said, bending down, hovering over him on her hands and knees, her dress still around her hips, the material dragging over him. The sensation of silk over his bare thighs must've gotten to him, because he went even harder.

She sat on his thighs, her dress covering him. Then she rested her palms on his biceps. "I love your arms, because they look like they could carry anything."

"They can carry you."

Yes, she wanted them to carry her everywhere, to places she'd never been before. Places only he could take her.

She skimmed her fingertips to his chest, where there was a fine dusting of dark blond hair. "I love how you look like a man, not a boy. How you take care of things like a man."

His chest was rising and falling with fast breaths, and he slipped his hands under her dress, hooked his thumbs into the sides of her panties, starting to lower them.

"As pleasant as this is," he said, grit in his tone, "I'm not going to last much longer."

"Just so you know how much I love every bit of you," she said. "Forever and always."

The last words had a tinge of foreboding to them, even though she hadn't meant it to be that way.

Hoping to erase it, she slid off of him, scooting back

to her pillows so she was still sitting up as he worked her undies from her body, tossing them to the floor.

Even as passion-steeped as she was, she remembered their baby, how to be safe, even while making love.

He rested his thumbs on her belly under her dress, his fingers splayed over her hips.

She wrapped her legs around him just as he entered her.

Mina made a primal sound of ultimate pleasure as he brought her to him, then away from him, their skin slick with sweat.

As they moved together, she saw circles in her mind—rings of fire that danced with flame, waving, touching her skin, charring it, kissing below the surface until she was branded deep down.

And the flames got bigger, higher, licking her faster and faster until she felt torched....

Higher, faster...pushed to her limits, fire in her, on her—

She flamed out in a series of tiny explosions that culminated in one big burst of heat, making her say his name.

But she didn't cool off yet. He wasn't done, and she stayed with him until he climaxed, too.

Then she held him close, refusing to let him go, hoping that he'd seen and felt a thousand truths in her love before she did what she had to do next....

They were still in bed, but even afterward, Chet sensed that Mina was more anxious than ever.

Did she think he was going to say, *Well, now that I got what I needed, I've changed my mind?*

Who could blame her if she did though? He'd put her through too much.

She came to rest on her side, facing him, that dress still on her, gathered at her waist, just above the sheets she'd pulled up, too. She had one hand under her pillow, the other under her chin, making her seem so vulnerable.

He touched the tip of her nose, her cheek, but didn't say anything.

Her eyes were wide when she started to talk. "Do you know when I first fell in love with you?"

He thought for a second, but he wasn't sure he knew the answer. Mina had always been Mina, never changing.

"Tell me," he said softly.

She smiled, but it was a tiny bit sad. He wasn't sure why. Wasn't sure what was going on with her at all.

"When you first walked through your office door," she said.

His heart jammed upward. "It was love at first sight?"

"You say it like you don't believe in it."

"I'm not sure I do. There's lust at first sight." And he'd never felt that for his assistant until the night he'd first gone to her for comfort, seeing something else in her entirely that had only grown to what it was now. Love.

"I know," she said. "It seems that love is too complex for it to happen in the first instant. That's what they say, anyway. But I'm not so sure about that. I think love's very simple." She wound her hand into his, wrapping her fingers, twining. "There you were, in a new business suit and your cowboy hat. It was your smile that got me, though. It flipped my heart right around, and I thought,

'This is the man. This is the one I've been waiting for.' I knew it without a doubt."

Chet wasn't certain if it was possible that a heart could crack, but his seemed to be doing it. In a nice way, too.

She went on, but there was still something in her voice that he couldn't identify.

"From just a look, I could tell so many things about you.... That you were pure-hearted. That you were a straight shooter." Her voice lowered. "That you expected people to be the same way with you."

"That's what I thought about you the first day, too."

"It was hard," she said, "working with you day in and day out, trying to hide my feelings."

"Is that why you never went out with anyone, because of me?"

"Pretty much. When you feel about someone the way I feel about you, it seems tawdry to be with another person, no matter how low the chances are of success with your true love."

What she was telling him was so sweet that he wanted to take hold of it. She was so unlike everything else in his life.

He began to pull her toward him, but she grabbed his wrist. He could feel her unsteadiness.

"I just wanted you to know that I've loved you more than anyone could ever love another person, Chet."

This was starting to sound...

Like a warning?

"What's wrong, Mina?" he asked.

She closed her eyes, as if she was gathering every bit of strength she had. As the seconds passed, it felt like daggers in his skin.

Finally, she opened her eyes again, pushing the dress down the rest of the way over her hips, discarding it.

Taking him by the hand and placing it on her belly.

"Chet," she said in a quivering voice, "we're going to have a baby."

Chapter Eleven

The announcement rang in Mina's ears for what seemed like a full minute as she watched Chet for a reaction.

Would he turn on her for keeping this a secret from him?

Had she told him too late…

…or still too *early?*

"A baby," he said, as if it hadn't quite sunk in yet.

She tightened her hold on his hand, which was still on her bare belly.

"A baby," she repeated, her heart throbbing in her ears.

Just as she thought she might not be able to take another breath, a smile broke out over Chet's face. And his eyes…

They were shining, welling with what she thought might be incredible, glinting joy.

Then he laughed, hugging her to him, putting his

hand right back on her tummy. At the same time, he was kissing her forehead, cradling her, and now it took *her* a few moments to process his response.

He wasn't mad at her....

She held to him, hardly believing that it could be this easy. He stroked her hair, and for a while it seemed as if this would go on for hours.

Then the moment she'd been dreading arrived.

As he still hugged her close, he rested his chin on her head. Her hand was over his heart, and she thought she could feel his pulse underneath her palm.

The slowing of its rhythm.

His silence cut into her, because the surprise had clearly passed for him. Reality had set in.

She didn't want to look up, into his eyes. But she did.

And what she saw shot her into pieces.

The moonlight revealed shadows—the ones that she thought had gone by the wayside already.

Sorrow flooded her. "Chet?"

"It had to have happened all those months ago," he said, almost as if to himself. "That night I came to your apartment."

"Yes."

He didn't go on, but she knew just what he had to be thinking.

"You're going to say that you wore a condom," she said. "But I'm pretty sure it broke. Afterward, both of us weren't paying as much attention to it as we should have—there was so much else going on." With her still trying to comfort him about the scandal and everything. "And I didn't find out for certain that I was pregnant until fairly recently. I wanted to tell you right away, but…"

He had come to touch her belly again, looking down at the place where their child was growing. "But you wanted to see how things would go with me and my family before you said anything. You thought I might take the news badly."

She didn't even know if she should say yes, so she didn't move, just waiting for him to go on instead.

He let go of her, and she scooted from him a few inches. They merely lay there for a while, next to each other, and soon he put his hand on her tummy again, as if he wanted the baby to know that he or she wasn't responsible for this tension.

The quiet was excruciating, because Mina knew that all Chet's demons had arrived, whispering in his ear.

An illegitimate baby, just like you, they had to be saying. *History repeating itself.*

But this wouldn't be a forbidden baby. Or an accident.

Didn't he realize that Mina had lived through the same sort of scenario and she would never allow a child to suffer because of the way he or she had been conceived?

That wasn't the worst part, though. Those demons would also be driving home to Chet that Mina hadn't let him in on the secret until now, after she had already known for a bit.

Keeping the truth from him would be just the same as a lie in his book.

What should've been the most wonderful moment of their lives was quickly going dark as the night collapsed around them. What made it worse was that she didn't even know what to say now, while he was so lost in his own mind and emotions.

At least his fingertips were *still* on her tummy, as if he'd already fallen in love with his child.

Was it only the mom he was angry at?

Her?

And she knew why he might be disappointed in her, too, even if she didn't know how to remedy it.

"I'm not like your mother," Mina said.

"I'd rather not talk about her right now."

Sure. He was going back into that shell of his, just as he'd done after the scandal had reared its ugly head.

But she wasn't about to let that happen.

"Just today," she said, "you told me that you knew you'd made a mistake in how you handled Eli. Now you're going to deal with me the same—"

"Please don't, Mina."

It would've hurt her less if it'd been an actual slap. As it was, she felt the mortifying sting of it.

She pulled the sheets up over her chest, and that forced his hand away from her and the baby.

Already, she felt abandoned.

"Okay," she said. "I'll leave it alone then. But we're going to have to talk about this sometime."

"I just want to..." He was staring at the ceiling. "Jeez, I don't want this to matter—the way the baby was conceived."

It went unsaid, but she knew he was mulling over how she'd presented the news to him—belatedly. Maybe even, according to him, cruelly.

"But it does matter," she said, so eager to get past this if he would let them.

She rose up to a kneeling position, still covering herself with the sheets. His hands seemed so empty as he rested them on his stomach.

"I want to hear everything you have to say," she said. "I want you to lay it all out there so we can take care of it now, not later, after it's had time to fester. Tell me what's going on with you."

He pressed his lips together.

"Please," she said.

Then he sent her a long glance that she couldn't quite understand, sat up, got out of the bed to put on his pants. She hadn't meant to drive him away—not tonight.

But she couldn't live with a partner who resented her, either.

"Is this about lying?" she asked.

"I..." He dug a hand into his hair. "Damn it, Mina, I just have to wonder how long you would have waited to tell me."

"Until I thought you could handle the news. And maybe I should've waited even longer, until after your wounds with Eli had mended a little more."

"You didn't trust me." What might've sounded petulant from another man only seemed rock-hard coming from him, as if his reaction had been written in stone a long time ago and it'd been fruitless to try to change it, even for her, the woman he supposedly loved.

She swallowed, clutching those sheets now.

All she could say was, "You can't compare this to what your mother did. I would never have done that to you. It's not even remotely the same."

But Mina could see that no matter how happy he'd seemed when he'd first heard the news, as the reality had set in, so had the hurt.

* * *

His mind was popping with so many different things, right or wrong, that he didn't know what to think.

There was genuine joy at the baby they were going to have, and that's what had come out when she'd announced the news.

But then there was the resentment that had followed—an emotion he didn't want to have, even though it wouldn't leave him.

He'd thought he'd gotten over his trials and tribulations, but here he was, still a prisoner of them.

But there was something *else* eating away at him that he hadn't expected, a dark mass that was just now taking shape.

He recalled when Mina had told him about her ex-boyfriend back at the Utah resort. How she'd said her family had despised the other guy after the break up.

In light of that, had she worried about bringing Chet, the father of her child, home? Had she ever wondered how her all-important family was going to react to the Barron bastard who couldn't be any good for her, either?

Had she been embarrassed about who he was and how that would affect her and their child?

They were over-the-top thoughts, but he couldn't help thinking them. He'd gone through too much rejection—just like the illegitimate child that Eli had never claimed until he'd been forced to do so. Just like the man who'd been lied to his entire life.

And Mina had lied to him, too.

She wrapped the sheets around her even more, covering all the skin she could, and that slammed him hard, as if she was retreating from him when, just shortly before, they'd been as together as two people could be.

With a child besides.

He thought of the moment he'd heard the news, and it folded him up inside, warm and bright.

They were going to have a baby.

He told himself to go back to her right now, to talk this out. But he'd been optimistic before and look where it'd gotten him.

Nowhere.

Maybe he just needed time.... Maybe it'd just be best to get out of here so he could breathe and think....

"This was what I was afraid of," Mina said from the bed.

She was pushing him and he wasn't in any place to tolerate it.

"You didn't think I'd be angry?" he asked. "Especially after you let me make love to you again? Were you buttering me up?"

Manipulating him?

He'd been manipulated enough.

"No," she said so forcefully that he immediately regretted the questions.

Then, softer, she said, "I knew you would be angry with me, and I deserve that. There were so many times I almost told you about the baby, but each moment never seemed right."

He wondered if his mother and Eli had ever talked together, asking themselves when the time would be right to let Chet in on their secret.

He *wanted* to be angry with Mina—it would feel so much better if he could direct it somewhere besides the vague world around him—but if there was a rational side of him, it was screaming that he would've been wary of sending a bombshell like this his way, too.

And he hated himself all the more for it.

Good God, what the hell kind of father would he be?

What had they gotten this baby into?

He was so livid that he wished there was a way to tell their baby that, no matter what, he or she would be protected. There'd never be ugliness because of his or her parents.

And that was why he put on the rest of his clothing, thinking that he really *should* cool off, weighing what to say to Mina next before he said something he couldn't take back.

"Where are you going?" she asked.

"To get myself together. It's not good for me to be here right now."

"Oh."

She said it as if he'd proven something, and good or bad, Chet actually felt as if she was accusing him of being a terrible father already. That she'd known he was going to blow it, and *that* was the reason she'd put off telling him.

He should've thought twice about that, but his nerves were shredded from all the scrapes they'd been getting into these past months.

"What does 'oh' mean?" he asked, even while knowing that he should've just left it alone.

He wanted to hear her say it, just as she'd wanted him to talk this out instead of just appreciating that they were going to have a baby together.

He added, "Did you think I'd walk out that door and never come back?"

When she flashed an injured gaze at him, he realized that Mina was dealing with her own issues here, too—the woman who'd never quite believed that people wouldn't reject *her.*

That dug into him even more.

"You actually did think that," he said, hardly believing it. "You thought I might be the kind of man who'd turn his back on his child, just like Eli did."

"No." But even though she tried to deny it, he could see it on her face.

Bam. Right in the gut.

The real truth.

His mind grasped at what was going on here because he just wasn't sure anymore.

Would she *always* be thinking that he would leave?

In spite of all the I-love-you's, did she actually trust him?

Crushed, he buttoned his shirt, put on his jacket. Now he *really* needed to cool off.

"Don't walk out that door," she said, her voice cracking.

"Don't worry, Mina." His heart felt as if it'd been sliced up and was stretching, trying like hell to bring itself back together. But it wasn't working. "You're afraid that I'd leave the baby behind, but in spite of what you might think of me, that's not the case. I'll always take care of my child."

She dropped back to lean against the wall, cocooned in that sheet, clearly decimated at what he'd said.

He would take care of the baby.

But what about her?

He left the question behind him, taking his battered

heart instead as he walked out of the cottage to do that cooling off he so sorely required.

Little did he know that when he returned she would be gone.

The morning after, Mina stared at the dawn-grayed ceiling of her house, the expanse of pale paint like a blank slate.

When Chet had left her in the cottage, she'd been so angry at him that she hadn't stayed, heading straight home in one of the Barrons' limos without Chet's knowledge. She'd felt too numb in the chest, just like another blank slate, this one marked with slashes of pain that only emphasized the otherwise empty expanse inside of her.

She had turned off her phone so Chet couldn't reach her and, once home, impulsively written a resignation letter to the Barron Group, hopping in her car and driving to the closed offices, where she'd slid the paper under his door, then left.

This morning, she'd still been angry at him, but she felt the same way with herself, too. It was just that she'd been hoping for a miracle, hoping that Chet wouldn't just say all the right things but that he would somehow banish how he really felt, as well.

Had she driven him away for good?

Now, as she kept looking at the ceiling, she formed another version of her resignation letter, one she could have sent.

Dear Sirs:

Much to my regret, I'm resigning my position at The Barron Group forthwith.

Working there would mean pretending that my boss, the man I thought I'd marry and be with for the rest of my life, still loved me. I'm not sure I could bear seeing him day after day.

She wiped a hand over her eyes, blocking her view of the ceiling. The real letter had been much more formal and professional, just as she'd always been. And she was clinging to the orderly, people-pleasingly simple Mina now, because she wasn't sure she had much more than that left.

Sitting up, she glanced at the old-school yellow phone on her secondhand coffee table, just as if that would make the thing ring. As if that would bring his voice on the other end of the line and he would beg her not only to come back to the office, but to return to him.

Yet she doubted that would happen, especially after what she'd said to him. He obviously hadn't *wanted* her enough to stay and, this time, it had been no accident.

This time, she'd earned the rejection because she'd wanted too much, too soon.

In fact, she feared that the only time she might hear from Chet was through an attorney, informing her that he was filing for custody.

Maybe she was overreacting, but that didn't mean the mere thought hadn't kept her up last night.

Tearfully, she rubbed her belly, wishing it was bigger, that her baby would be coming sooner.

Wishing she didn't want to take back the last couple of weeks to see if things could've turned out differently.

"I'm such a whiz," said Mina's father that same afternoon as they sat in the living room of her parents' home, avoiding the overcast weather outside. Since she'd been up and about since the crack of dawn, she'd come here early, needing the company.

The change in temperature had triggered some kind of cold in her dad, and his nose was stuffy, the scent of VapoRub wafting from him.

"This almost makes me forget that I'm not on the high seas with your mother," he said while he toyed with the new smartphone that Amy and her husband had purchased for him as a birthday gift. It did seem to cheer him up, because even though he'd pretended that he wasn't looking forward to the cruise, his sickness had caused her parents to miss it. They weren't even going to have a big impromptu party for his birthday tomorrow because he needed to rest.

Mina smiled at his interest in the phone, but her gesture wasn't natural. She had so many "wired up" devices herself—her own smartphone, her computer, the iPad—and even though they were supposed to connect a person with the rest of the world, Mina didn't feel linked to much of anyone at all, except for the baby.

To make things even worse, her dad's enthusiasm reminded her of Chet's level of expertise with newfangled "doodads."

Then again, everything reminded her of Chet.

Surely he'd read her letter by now, but did he even care? There'd been no phone calls from him—only a few from her friends in the office who'd checked in about her absence and learned of her resignation. Danny and Corrine had even invited her out to dinner tonight to say goodbye.

The aroma of chicken soup floated through the room,

and Mina's mom came out of the kitchen, carrying a couple of bowls with steam waving out of them.

"Eat up," Mom said, slipping a serving in front of Mina on the pine coffee table just before she gave one to Dad, too.

"I'm not that hungry." Her stomach was a mess because she hadn't just come here to nurse her dad.

She had some things to get off of her chest if she wanted to move on without Chet. To do that, she knew that her support system would help to pull her through.

True, she knew she could survive without interference from her family, but it felt darn good to have it if she wanted it.

Mom was spooning some of the soup and lifting it to Mina's mouth.

"Seriously, Mom," Mina said. "Not hungry."

"All right, crankypants." Her mother frowned as she put the spoon back into the bowl.

Dad laughed under his breath.

"Chicken soup is proven to lift moods as well as fight sickness," Mom said to him. "I could eat a whole pot of it along with ten bars of chocolate some days." She patted her stomach. "I'd pay for it, though."

"Honey," Dad said, "if there's more of you to love, I won't be complaining."

"Thank you, Ewan." Mom rolled her eyes.

Dad seemed to know just when to leave a room…and a woman's mild temper. He got up from his chair and headed for the hallway.

"I might get better reception back here," he said, pointing to his phone.

"You sure will." Mom still wasn't over his food comment.

Mina grinned at him as he disappeared, his slippers leaving soft footfalls on the carpet.

"I swear," she said, sitting back on the couch. "Years of marriage, and it's like he still hasn't figured out that I'm touchy when it comes to weight. There are just some things you don't say to a woman."

Mina pressed her lips together. There were some things you didn't say to a man, either, but she'd said them to Chet.

"Sometimes," she whispered, "we say things we don't mean." *And sometimes there's a big cost.* "Dad was actually being sweet to you, Mom."

She smiled a bit. "So he was."

Her dad had turned on the TV back in his room, and the murmur of it imitated the muddled noise in Mina's heart. It wouldn't quiet itself.

"So what's wrong?" Mom asked.

It wouldn't do to avoid the question. She'd come over here for that tender love and care, so why not admit it?

But it was the lingering shame of displeasing her mom with her behavior that made it hard to speak right now. Her parents had raised her to be a good girl, and Mina had been wondering about how they would react to her sleeping with another man outside of a committed relationship. It'd been bad enough with Michael.

Yet hadn't her mom told her she was independent? Hadn't she sounded as if she respected that, too?

Mina realized that, like Chet, she needed to put her family matters in order once and for all if she was going to go forward.

She steadied herself, then said, "I'm pregnant, Mom."

The moment her mother put her hands over her mouth and her eyes lit up, Mina broke open with a tiny sob she'd been holding back ever since things had gone to hell with Chet.

"Oh, sweetie!"

Mom hugged her, rocking her back and forth as the tears really started to come.

Pregnancy hormones. But crying was also profound relief, a load off of Mina's shoulders.

"When are you due?" Mom asked, looking at Mina, wiping the tears from her daughter's eyes, even as she cried herself.

"In about four months."

"And...Chet? I assume he's..."

Mina could only nod while her mom stroked the hair back from her face. She was sobbing now, an obvious signal that things were not going well with the father.

"What happened?" her mom asked softly.

It felt good to have an ally, and Mina told her almost everything—about the night Chet had found out about his illegitimacy, about how they'd gotten together, then closer and closer, until she'd dropped the news on him.

She almost expected her mom to say something about how Mina needed to stop picking guys who didn't deserve her, but instead, she got something else altogether.

"So when are you two going to patch this up?"

The surety in her mom's tone made Mina look up and say, "You're not going to give me 'the talk'?"

"Like the one you got last time?"

Mina nodded.

Her mom tucked Mina's hair behind her ear. "Sweetie, Michael was an engaging guy, but he was one of those slackers. There are little details that reveal everything about a man, and when I saw how he loved to be waited on hand and foot and how he disengaged from the family to sit here and watch TV while we'd sit out on the porch with each other… Well, that spoke volumes." She shook her head. "Chet felt real, though. A mother knows these things."

Mina almost started crying again.

"Have you talked to him at all?" her mom asked, saving her.

"No. I've wanted to call him, but…I'm afraid."

"Of what?"

Mina held up her palms. "What if he's always going to be angry with me for not trusting him?" Sorrow pushed up through her chest, making her words tangled. "I wouldn't be able to stand it. It'd be concrete evidence that he never cared that much in the first place. He's already put me aside, even though he promised to always take care of the baby."

Mom held Mina's face in her hands. "Your child deserves every chance you can give him or her. You've got to talk to Chet."

"I know. It's the most important thing in the world to do, especially for the baby's sake." She bit her lip, as if it would hold back everything else she wanted to say, but it didn't work. "Among other matters, children should never feel as if their parents didn't want them."

Empathy changed her mother's expression. She was obviously thinking about the circumstances of Mina's birth.

"I've known about it for years, Mom," Mina said.

"Uncle Dennis was drunk once, and I heard him talk about it during one of our family get-togethers. I just never told you."

"Oh, Mina." She stroked her daughter's hair again.

"It's no big tragedy. I mean, I grew up fine."

"But it's something no child should hear." Her smile was soft, like a mother's should be. "Your father and I weren't sure that we could afford to have any other children at that time. But there you were, in spite of any precautions we took."

She'd already known the circumstances, but she touched her belly, anyway, as if her baby could hear. As if shielding him or her from all of this.

"We started celebrating you right away, Mina," her mom added. "And it kills me to think that we might not have had you at all but for an 'accident.'" She touched Mina's cheek. "*Accident.* What a word for it when, really, it was as if someone or something out there was telling us that you needed a home, and we were the lucky ones who were chosen to bring you in to one. And there hasn't been a moment when we haven't thanked our stars for you."

Did you hear that? Mina asked her child. *That's exactly how I feel about you.*

"I could just throttle Uncle Dennis," her mom said, narrowing her eyes. "He had no business talking about that when we told him in confidence."

"It's okay," Mina said.

Because it was.

It really was.

It'd been a long time in coming, but hearing her mother say this with tears in her eyes made all the difference.

And it caused Mina to realize that *she* was going to be a mother. Really and truly a mother. She genuinely felt just how devastating it would be to not have been blessed with someone who was going to bring such joy into her life.

She understood so much now.

But what about the father of her baby?

Would he still consider Mina an accident…

…or was he thinking about her as much as she was pining away for him?

Chapter Twelve

Hours later that same day, Chet sat in the stables at Florence Ranch, holding a copy of Mina's resignation letter in his hands while sitting on a bale of hay. He'd cut out early from the office for some peace and quiet, because his mind sure wasn't giving him any rest.

He still couldn't forget the look that had been on Mina's face when he'd left her. It was as if he'd pulled the floor out from under her, and gradually, realization—and betrayal—had taken over her expression. Then he'd stupidly left her alone, just to do that cooling off thing of his, only to come back and find everything gone—her luggage, her clothing…

Her.

Then, even more foolishly, he'd told himself that she just needed a little space, so he hadn't called her, believing that he would see her this morning when he reported for work on a rare late day at the office, where they could find some time alone together to smooth things over.

And that was when he'd found the letter under his door.

A remote, polite, businesslike resignation from his life.

That was when he realized that a mere phone call wasn't going to erase the words they'd said to each other.

Unless he proved otherwise, was she always going to think he was too troubled?

He needed some advice on this, so he had come back here to the ranch to…

Hell, he might as well admit it. For the first time, he needed his brothers, and he'd left word back at the mansion asking them to meet him here.

He folded the letter while next to him in a stall, an Arabian mare stomped her hoof and nickered. Chet stood, just about ready to put the paper into his business suit pocket when someone walked through the entrance to the stables.

Scratch that—it was two people. Tyler and Jeremiah, who hadn't left on his honeymoon with Ally to Lake Arrowhead in California yet.

"Saddling up?" Jeremiah asked Chet, eyeing his business suit.

"I didn't want to go in the mansion, so that's why I'm here instead."

Since Eli hadn't gone back to rehab yet, Chet had wanted to avoid the big house and any talk about Mina with his father. Besides, he'd already said goodbye to Eli this morning, before he'd headed out for the office.

It looked as if Jeremiah and Tyler were ready to ride

themselves, with their jeans and hats. They were watching him expectantly. Everyone on the ranch knew that Mina had left already—Chet had only told them she'd scheduled an early day at the Group—and his hangdog expression was probably causing his brothers to wonder just *what* was going on.

Might as well get this over with.

Chet held up the letter. "Mina quit the Group."

Jeremiah nodded. "When I checked in with my assistant an hour ago, she told me. Some of the staff is going to be meeting Mina tonight to see what's going on with her, why she's leaving. I suspect some might even want to make a play at changing her mind."

Tyler stepped in. "Why did she quit, Chet?"

"We had…a falling out last night. And I'm afraid it was mostly because of my damned issues."

Tyler exhaled loudly.

"What's that mean?" Chet asked, immediately realizing that he was about to get his first real brother-to-brother-to-brother talk about something that had nothing to do with Eli.

Tyler said, "I won't presume to play big brother to you unless you're willing to hear it."

Jeremiah lifted an eyebrow to Chet, seconding Tyler's comment.

Chet didn't know where it came from, but he got one of those warm glows in his chest that he mainly felt when it seemed that Mina was watching over him, doing anything for him.

He'd hoped that he might have two brothers who'd do the same for him, except…

Well, this was different. They were family, not a partner.

"What do you have to say, Ty?"

Just like the Group leader he'd been for years before he quit, the oldest Barron dove straight in. "The way I see it, we were all given a mighty dose of bad medicine to swallow these past several months. I was ready to tear Eli apart with my bare hands for what he'd done. As for Jeremiah…I guess you could say he got a little lost, himself."

"Hey," Jeremiah said, with a smile. "I got found."

"And that's my point," Tyler said. "We had certain someones come into our lives at exactly the right time, just like answers to prayers. I don't know how I would've managed without Zoe."

"Ditto here, but with Ally, of course," Jeremiah said. "And I think I know where Ty is going with this. There were times when we both almost ruined what Zoe and Ally brought to the table for us when we needed it the most."

"But they're strong women," Tyler said, "and they took our guff. Each one of them is capable of that, Chet."

"Including Mina." Jeremiah had that eyebrow cocked again as he measured his younger brother.

Chet kept holding that letter. Damn it, he still loved her. He always would.

Would they know how to dig him out of this hole?

Chet pushed up the brim of his hat. "If I knew how to fix what I've done to Mina, I'd have made things right with her already. But what we have is more than just a simple misunderstanding."

"What's the problem then?" Tyler asked.

"She's pregnant. That's not a problem, though."

Both men had skipped right over that last part, dwelling on the baby news.

"Congratulations," Tyler and Jeremiah said at the same time, lighting up, and it seemed as if they were about to come forward to shake Chet's hand.

But then Chet told them the rest: how Mina had apparently seriously considered the consequences of being with someone like him—just as undependable as the last man who'd broken her heart. How she thought he might feel about his own illegitimate child, what with being one himself.

"I don't even know where it all started going downhill," Chet finished. "Where we began to argue and say the wrong things to each other."

Jeremiah had come to stand with his hands planted on his hips. "Did you tell her you'd never have her raise a child alone?"

"Of course." Chet crumpled the letter a little in his hand. "I told her that I'd always take care of the baby, but I was so taken aback by what we said to each other that I didn't say I'd take care of *her.* And I want to do that. I can't imagine a future without her."

"Damn," Tyler said. "I never realized it before, but for a mellow man, you're really bullheaded, Chet."

"I don't want to be."

Jeremiah said, "Listen, I made my mistakes with Ally, too, and I would've ended up crawling back to her on my hands and knees if I'd needed to. Luckily, it didn't come to that."

"You've got to stop thinking about everything bad that might happen," Tyler said, getting back into leadership mode, "and think about what good might come out of it instead."

Chet just stared at his oldest brother. When the scandal had broken, Tyler would've been the last person on earth to be talking in optimistic terms.

Taking a chance with Zoe had changed him though, just as Ally had done for Jeremiah.

The only difference between Chet and them was that they'd been strong enough to take a risk, to put their hearts on the line.

And he wanted to be like his brothers, a Barron through and through. But, even more importantly, he wanted Mina.

Chet appealed to them. "You two won Zoe and Ally back...."

They seemed to understand that he was looking for ideas on how he could do it, too.

Jeremiah leaned against the stable wall as he said, "For starters, if you want to make an impression, we know where Mina's definitely going to be tonight."

Chet fisted her resignation paper in his hand, taking it from there.

When Mina walked into the steak house where she was to meet some of her ex-coworkers for dinner, she had the feeling something was up.

She moved past the moose heads over the main fireplace, stone walls and antler light fixtures, finding about ten friends seated at a long family-style table in a back room.

"Mina!" they shouted.

Danny patted her on the back as Corrine pulled out a chair at the head of the table for Mina to sit.

So many people here. Gratefulness bunched in her chest as she realized that they cared about her quitting the Group. But it pained her all the more, knowing that, evidently, Chet didn't give a fig. He hadn't called or anything.

And the longer *she* waited to do so, the harder it got.

"I'm sorry we didn't have the chance to work together longer," Danny said to her. "But I see big things in store for you in the future, Mina Ferguson."

"Thanks."

"Are you at least coming to the opening of the resort?"

"I'm afraid not."

Her stomach knotted. She'd nursed that project just as much as Chet had done, but she wouldn't be able to see it come to maturity. Yet she still had her real baby, though she wasn't sure if his or her dad would even be at *that* birth.

As she tried to still her falling heart, Danny took a seat nearby while the others—mainly assistants she'd come up through the ranks with—aimed questions her way about why she was leaving.

She gave all the right answers, about searching out bigger opportunities, etc., while big family-style sharing plates were set down on the table and the group dug in. They'd already ordered, and she smiled, thinking that everyone in the Barron Group was just as efficient as she was.

That they would be very much okay without her.

She peered out a nearby window at the early evening sky, plus the autumn-tinged trees…and the view of the tall, stately Barron Group offices in the near distance.

Far enough away so that she already felt as if she'd left them behind.

But had she?

She nibbled at a bread stick, looking around the table, realizing how much of her identity was tied up with the Group. It'd been a home to her, a challenging place to go where she could excel and feel proud of her accomplishments.

She'd been a people pleaser, but, damn it, she'd pleased herself an awful lot, too. And that had to be worth something.

When everyone at the table suddenly shifted their focus behind her, toward the entrance of the restaurant, then waved in surprised greeting, a shiver played down Mina's spine.

A wonderful shiver.

"Chet!" a few of them said.

She froze in her seat, hardly believing she was hearing his name.

His name, which flowed through her like warmed honey.

"Mina," said Chet's voice, and she didn't dare look back at him for fear of losing her composure in front of all these people she'd once worked with, once tried to fool by acting as if she wasn't head over heels in love with the boss.

No, she would explode into tears in front of everyone if she looked.

Now she could feel Chet standing behind her chair. There was heat on her neck, and it was slipping lower, sending her into a pool of longing.

Danny had stood, pulling out a chair. "Take a seat, sir."

"Thanks," Chet said. "But, all the same, I'd like to stay where I am for a minute."

Now everyone seemed to be watching Mina, probably wondering why she was blushing so furiously and why she wouldn't look at her former boss.

She slowly glanced up at him, and if she thought she'd been heated before, the crash of flame that hit her now just about knocked her out of her seat.

He was as handsome as ever, strong, stalwart while wearing his hat, plus a casual Western shirt and new jeans. He was carrying a tote bag that was weighed down by something, but he didn't show anyone what it was.

This was the Chet no one in the office really knew. This was *her* Chet, any way he dressed, because she knew him inside and out.

"Hi," she said softly, testing him, hoping to God he wouldn't just walk away from her again.

As he looked down at her, the background music was the only sound, save for the other diners and the clink of silverware against plates.

He doffed his hat, and she saw that his eyes were blue like an early Texas spring sky that was just on the edge of renewal.

When he spoke, he kept that gaze on her, even though he was talking to the rest of the group.

"Sorry for the interruption," he said, "but I wanted to take the opportunity to try and talk Mina into staying."

Everyone applauded at that, and each clap was like a chop to Mina.

Really, that was the reason he'd come here?

Because he'd lost his assistant and he wanted her back?

That couldn't be. Not after she'd seen what she'd seen in his eyes just now.

He held up his hand. "Everyone knows that I'm never going to find someone like Mina. Not anywhere."

His words carried a double meaning—business and personal—and suddenly his first words did, too.

I wanted to take the opportunity to try and talk Mina into staying.

With him?

He came to the side of her chair, so close that her hands began to quiver. She folded her arms over her tummy without really knowing she'd done it.

"I wish to God you would come back," he said to her, so low that his voice combed over her, owning her.

It was as if he'd forgotten what they'd said to each other last night, what had made them both angry in the first place.

And they couldn't ignore that.

She turned to him. "You think this is going to do it? Bring me back?"

"I'm hoping it's a start."

She realized that the whole table was getting uncomfortable. This had gone beyond a conversation about Chet wanting her to return to the Group, and they could obviously sense it.

But he didn't back off.

He wasn't running away this time or making up excuses to hide how they felt about each other.

"Imagine me," he said so everyone else could hear, "on my first day, walking into the Group's offices. I'd seen the place when I was a little boy, and it was hellishly imposing even then. But as a new co-vice president?" He shook his head. "It made me want to go back to Montana and never look back. But Mina took care of me. She ran my schedules, made sure I looked good every step of the way. I knew that she was going to go far in the Group, and she did. But, even as she was moving up that corporate ladder, there was a hitch."

The love he'd confessed for her last night was even clearer in his gaze now.

My Lord, she thought. He was about to come clean after stubbornly using and reusing that line about how much he didn't want to sully her reputation at the Group.

He was laying it *all* out there.

"I finally saw what was in front of me all along and fell in love with this woman," Chet said.

Everyone was silent, wide-eyed. Mina was the worst of them all as her breathing quickened, her gaze going hazy.

He loved her, even after everything.

Danny was the first one to rise from his chair, followed by Corrine.

"Er," he said. "I've got to..."

He pointed toward the restrooms. One by one, the rest of them followed, leaving their food for later.

Chet remained, though edgy, as if wary of how she was going to react.

"Why did you say all that in front of them?" she asked.

"They're going to know anyway that we were together, and I wanted to make it as clear as day that I won't tolerate any gossip about you...or us...or how you earned your way through the Group." He took her hand in his. "I wanted everyone to know how much I treasure you, Mina—not just as my assistant, but..."

He held her hand over his heart.

"But as the woman I want to be with forever and always."

Last night, Mina had told him that, too, and suddenly she didn't care that they were in a back room in a public place where anyone could walk in on them.

She was only a woman who wanted to go forward with the man she loved.

Mina's eyes had a glassy look that told Chet she was about to cry. And when he reached into the bag he was carrying, showing her what was in it, the tears came.

"Here," he said, giving her a thick pastel book that he'd purchased.

A how-to baby book.

She hugged it to her chest, lowering her head. Chet wanted to touch her, just a brush of his fingertips over her cheek. Just a skim over the beautiful auburn hair that gleamed in the lights.

But they weren't quite to that point yet.

"I want to be the best dad I can be," he said, his voice thick. "When I said I'll always be there for the baby, I meant it. It's just that I left out the most important part besides that."

"What?"

He took a chance, laid his hand on top of hers as she kept hugging that book.

"That I want to be there for you, too."

A tear wiggled down her cheek, and she reached up to whisk it away.

"I just wonder though," he said, "if you can bear with me while I learn to trust again. While I get the rest of my life together and leave all my baggage behind."

She nodded, but obviously couldn't say much more.

"Mina?"

"Sorry," she said with a croak. "I just get so emotional lately. I'm sure that's why I overreacted when I told you about the baby."

"You expected me to put my issues behind me. You weren't asking too much, even though it felt like it at the time."

He heard the words coming from him and marveled that he was able to say them.

But Mina had shown him how. Only Mina.

"I was wrong to expect that of you," she said. "I thought you were going to bolt right out the door, but I came to realize that I've got to trust you, too."

"You know I'm never going to hurt you again, right?"

She finally met his gaze, as if she knew that he was talking about her previous heartbreaks, not just the one they'd had together last night.

As if she already was willing to put all of her soul into trusting him.

The power of their visual connection would've sent him to his knees if he hadn't already intended to get down on one of them.

He lowered himself to the carpet, reaching into his back pocket, coming out with a velvet box. A ring he'd bought on the way over here, too.

Now Mina really started to cry.

"Be my wife?" he asked. "Keep on being the best partner I could've ever found?"

She knelt down, too. "Yes, yes, I will."

As a trill sang through him, he rested a hand on her tummy. She'd worn a baggy skirt, although she was still slender and the baby hadn't shown him or herself much at all.

But he still knew his son or daughter was in there.

"And you?" he asked their baby. "How do you feel about this?"

"He or she wants you to just put the ring on me," Mina said, laughing.

It felt so damned good to laugh with her as she slid the diamond-studded band onto her finger. It was a little loose, but it would do for now.

"We'll get it fitted," he said.

"It already fits just fine."

They embraced, kissed, as if finding each other again after too long of a separation.

Then, suddenly, Mina sucked in a breath, drawing way from him.

"Oh," she said, her hands flying to her belly.

"Are you okay?" His heart was palpitating like mad.

"Yes, it's..." She brought one of his hands to her tummy. "This is the first time I've felt anything. Can you feel the baby?"

He thought he did—a little thump that brought the idea of having a child with her to full life.

Overwhelmed, he kissed her again, and Mina leaned her forehead against his.

"We're going to have a little person," she said.

"Yeah."

"Did you know that, right now, this little person probably has hair on his or her head and might even be able to hear us?"

"Really?"

"Really."

Chet guided Mina back to a stand while he remained kneeling. He cupped her hips, pressing his lips to her tummy.

"Your mommy just made me the happiest man alive," he murmured against her, hoping the baby really could hear. "And you've only made me happier."

Mina rested her hands on Chet's head, all of them finally connected, father, mother and child.

Epilogue

"So when's it your turn, Ty?" Chet asked his brother as the family gathered in the grand living room in the Florence Ranch mansion months later.

Tyler looked down at Chet, who was sitting on a love seat next to Mina, holding his newborn son, Colin. Tufts of reddish hair were already peeking out from under his blue baby cap.

Tyler only grinned in answer to Chet's question while tickling Colin's cheek.

Mina laughed. "Evasive, Ty?"

She didn't look as if she'd been pregnant just a couple of weeks ago, but she did seem like a newlywed, three months married in a ceremony that the family had held here on the ranch, just like the rest of the Barrons.

Zoe wandered over from where Ally was holding court with Caroline. Mina's mom was holding the rosy-cheeked infant, and little Lizzie, who'd begged to come with her grandparents for the weekend to the ranch, was fussing with the red bow in the baby's hair. The Barrons had invited the Fergusons over, just like they did at least once a month these days.

While glancing up at Tyler, Zoe pulled on his shirt-sleeve. She had a playful look on her face.

By the time Ty got around to talking, Chet had already guessed the news.

"We *are* pregnant," his brother said.

From the other side of the room, Jeremiah gave one of his victory whoops, and everyone congratulated Tyler and Zoe at once.

But no one seemed more excited than Eli, who got out of his wingback chair and enveloped Tyler, then Zoe, in a hug.

Chet watched his father, smiling. Eli was about four months sober now. He attended his AA meetings while his sons attended their Al-Anon gatherings on a regular basis.

It was all working out for the Barrons now, but who would've guessed it all those months ago?

"How far are you along?" Mina asked Zoe.

"Three months. We want to wait until the birth to see what the sex will be, though. It'll be a nice surprise."

Chet slipped his hand into Mina's. That hadn't been the route they'd traveled. Soon after he'd proposed to her, they'd gone to their first doctor's appointment together, and they'd found out Colin's disposition. Chet had gone a little nuts afterward, shopping for baby boy stuff until Mina had told him that he was likely to fill a semitruck before he got through.

He'd even had a hand in putting the final touches on the day care center at the resort, and during its grand opening, Mina had been there, proud as could be as they'd looked upon what they'd created as partners.

And they were that in the truest sense of the word. She'd come back to the Group, opening the resort with Chet, staying on right up until she'd been ready to give birth. Now she was taking time off to be with Colin.

Actually, Chet had cut back on work, too, finding that there was no need for all the business trips he'd been engaged in. Not when he had so much to come home to every night.

Near a silver beverage service that had been brought in for their gathering, Eli used a ladle to transfer some of Lizzie's Woodland Punch to plastic party glasses. The little girl put herself in charge of giving everyone the drink for a toast to Ty and Zoe's pregnancy.

As Eli held his punch aloft, he led the salutation. "Here's to my sons," he said, his voice scratchy. "Miracles, every one of them. And here's to my new daughters, too."

"Here, here," said Mina's dad, clinking cups with his wife, then kissing her on a blushing cheek.

"And," Eli added, bending down to Lizzie, "here's to the traveling band we'll soon have if my sons and daughters keep going at the rate they are."

Lizzie probably didn't know what a traveling band was, but she joyfully clinked with Eli, anyway. It was obvious the old man adored her, especially in the ladybug-decorated early spring dress she'd chosen for today.

As everyone started throwing around possible names for a traveling band, Chet noticed that Colin had gotten heavy-lidded, so he rose from the love seat, pressing a kiss to Mina's forehead.

"I'm going to walk him around a little, get him to sleep."

"You do that, Daddy."

She smiled at him with such love that he could barely contain himself. But Colin was such a sound sleeper that Chet would be able to spend a lot of quality time tonight with his wife.

And many nights afterward.

Chet walked his son through the halls, past the ballroom and the windows with their flowery views of spring.

Finally, he came to the lounge.

To the new portrait that hung over the mantel.

The Barrons had commissioned an artist to recreate the original painting, with Eli, Aunt Florence, Tyler and Jeremiah posing so stoically in it.

But there'd been some additions.

Now the portrait held more Barrons, including Abe, Chet's mom…

…and Chet.

He didn't feel like a ghost anymore, and he knew that, in time, he was going to have a picture of his own family in a place of honor in his home. Colin would see himself in it, along with any future brothers and sisters, and he would know that he had always been accounted for.

Always wanted.

He heard footsteps behind him and turned to see Mina entering the room. She came to him, slid her arms around his waist, rested her chin against his arm so she could look down on the baby, who was slumbering away.

They could've made for a beautiful portrait right

now—a family who'd made it through bad times to get to the good.

A family united forever and always.

* * * * *

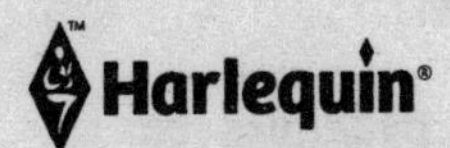

SPECIAL EDITION®

COMING NEXT MONTH

Available June 28, 2011

#2125 RESISTING MR. TALL, DARK & TEXAN
Christine Rimmer
Montana Mavericks: The Texans are Coming!

#2126 TO HAVE THE DOCTOR'S BABY
Teresa Southwick
Men of Mercy Medical

#2127 THE DOCTOR TAKES A PRINCESS
Leanne Banks

#2128 HER FILL-IN FIANCÉ
Stacy Connelly

#2129 HOW TO LASSO A COWBOY
Christine Wenger
Gold Buckle Cowboys

#2130 IT'S NEWS TO HER
Helen R. Myers

HSECNM0611

USA TODAY *bestselling author B.J. Daniels takes you on a trip to Whitehorse, Montana, and the Chisholm Cattle Company.*

RUSTLED

Available July 2011 from Harlequin Intrigue.

As the dust settled, Dawson got his first good look at the rustler. A pair of big Montana sky-blue eyes glared up at him from a face framed by blond curls.

A woman rustler?

"You have to let me go," she hollered as the roar of the stampeding cattle died off in the distance.

"So you can finish stealing my cattle? I don't think so." Dawson jerked the woman to her feet.

She reached for the gun strapped to her hip hidden under her long barn jacket.

He grabbed the weapon before she could, his eyes narrowing as he assessed her. "How many others are there?" he demanded, grabbing a fistful of her jacket. "I think you'd better start talking before I tear into you."

She tried to fight him off, but he was on to her tricks and pinned her to the ground. He was suddenly aware of the soft curves beneath the jean jacket she wore under her coat.

"You have to listen to me." She ground out the words from between her gritted teeth. "You have to let me go. If you don't they will come back for me and they will kill you. There are too many of them for you to fight off alone. You won't stand a chance and I don't want your blood on my hands."

"I'm touched by your concern for me. Especially after you just tried to pull a gun on me."

HIEXP0711R

"I wasn't going to shoot you."

Dawson hauled her to her feet and walked her the rest of the way to his horse. Reaching into his saddlebag, he pulled out a length of rope.

"You can't tie me up."

He pulled her hands behind her back and began to tie her wrists together.

"If you let me go, I can keep them from coming back," she said. "You have my word." She let out an unladylike curse. "I'm just trying to save your sorry neck."

"And I'm just going after my cattle."

"Don't you mean your boss's cattle?"

"Those cattle are mine."

"*You're* a Chisholm?"

"Dawson Chisholm. And you are…?"

"Everyone calls me Jinx."

He chuckled. "I can see why."

Bronco busting, falling in love…it's all in a day's work.
Look for the rest of their story in

RUSTLED

Available July 2011 from Harlequin Intrigue
wherever books are sold.

HIEXP0711R